I'm a fai
female.

MW01206318

Twins are alphas. Full. Stop. It's a given.

Only, with my first shift came proof I'd built my future on assumptions. My sister presented alpha immediately, but me? I'm nothing but an omega. It was fine. Really it was…until it wasn't.

On my eighteenth birthday, my pack emerged, drawn to me by my scent, the perfume of a newly blossomed omega. Their decision was made in seconds. They rejected me in favor of my taller, more beautiful, more alpha sister.

She accepted my pack as her own, not even pretending to give it a thought. Without a mate, I'm a liability and, since presenting, my family treats me as such. I'm their maid. Their cook. Their embarrassment. I was once one of their princesses.

Now I'm something that needs to be put out, like the trash. They prove that point by selling me to the first pack that will take a weak omega like me—the DarkShadow Pack.

I've heard of them—the whispers, the stories told in the dark—the secrets. They're a pack of ruthless brutes who don't deal well with others and aren't strangers to the shifter judicial system. No omega in her right mind would accept them, but I don't have a choice. It's either them or death. Please let me have made the right choice.

Knot Our Omega is the first in the Stuck in a Rut shifter why choose sweetverse romances. Each stand-alone novel features an omega female and her brutish, brooding wolf shifter alphas. Knot Our Omega features an omega strong enough to tame the wildest beast, the dream that leads them to find their mate and empty their bank account, a misunderstood pack, omegaverse goodies including heat, rutting, marking, perfuming, slick, and all the knotty goodness you love.

And of course, a happy ever after that includes an adorable baby or two.

Knot Our Omega

Digital ISBN: 979-8-89320-129-1

Print ISBN: 979-8-89320-130-7

Published by Decadent Publishing LLC

Knot Our Omega

A Wolf Shifter Sweetverse Romance

By

Mazzy J. March

And Ever Knottington

Chapter One

Rumor

"You better hurry up, Rumor." One of my parents' house omegas, Lily, whispered low, only for me. "You don't want today to go…you know."

You know, meaning, my parents would give out consequences and not to me. No. They would never lay a hand on me because they knew it would look bad upon the alpha house. Instead, they would pick one of the house omegas, preferably one I was friendly with, and bleed them slowly in front of me and the others as a lesson.

Fuck that noise.

They chose more demeaning ways to punish me. By adding things to my daily chores like toilet cleaning or cleaning out the trash cans. Things I hadn't ever been trained for.

I was trained and raised to be an alpha, like my twin sister Reyna. Until everything changed.

"I just need to get my hair tied back." And it had to be perfect. I wasn't allowed to have a strand of it out of my braid. My mother said the braid showed that I wasn't a lowly servant, even though I was doing servant work. It didn't.

And I was the lowliest in this family. Everyone else in this house was an alpha or an alpha's mate.

"I'll help." Lily worked quickly and we were downstairs in the kitchen getting ready for tonight's dinner.

My twin sister convinced my parents to have a "dinner party," something she saw on a human television show. She said it would be "fun," but really she meant, it would show the pack that she was powerful and important, which she was. Our larger pack and her pack. Her harem. Men who treated her like royalty. Men who were supposed to be mine.

She paraded her power and prestige any chance she got.

Once upon a time, I was too. Powerful and mighty despite my shorter stature. Twin alphas born to the alpha family was the stuff of hierarchy dreams. Only I

2

wasn't an alpha at all, presenting as omega for the first time on my eighteenth birthday. Happy fucking birthday to me.

They say a parent's love is unconditional and that twins share a connection like no other. They lie. The second my perfume tickled a local pack member's nose, my parents locked me away and turned me into nothing more than a glorified servant—heavy on the servant, low on the glorified.

They never failed to remind me that my place in this family was shaky.

"How many are coming?" The list of food we had to make for the evening was missing a head count. Did they expect me to guess? Setting me up to fail? Honestly, at this point, nothing would surprise me. My family was determined to make me as small as possible—a whisper of a person.

"All of them?" Lily uncovered the commercial mixer. "And they want fresh bread, of course."

"All…as in the entire pack?"

Lily nodded. "And they pulled the other servants to work on…they didn't say what."

3

Odds were, they were pulled for nothing, and this was a test. Not for Lily. She was there because they needed someone's safety to hold over my head, and she was the closest to my age and as sweet as the cupcakes I made for dessert.

She deserved a pack to treat her as the queen she was. All omegas did. Lily had been the one to teach me about perfuming and about scent blockers. She said the rest would be saved for when I got a pack.

"Let's do this thing." It wasn't worth discussing. It wasn't as if we had the ability to change any of this.

Hours later, we had everything prepped or cooked and the table set. All that was left was the serving. I was getting pretty good at cooking and didn't mind it as a rule, but this meal had been labor-intensive, even for an army of omegas. They wanted too much made in too short a period of time with too few ovens. As if they were intentionally setting me up to fail.

The harsh reality was, that might be exactly what they were doing.

Everyone arrived on time—exactly. My parents expected it, and the pack obeyed. I wasn't the only one

4

they were shitty to. I wish I had seen how bad it was when I was younger, back when I had the potential to make a difference.

Lily and I served the dinner, standing to the side to clear empty plates, fill drinks, and offer seconds. We were to be invisible while on top of things. It was an impossible expectation, but one I'd gotten better at over the years.

"The dinner is lovely." My sister set her fork down, looking around to make sure all eyes were on her before adding, "Rumor has become quite the little baker."

"I agree. She's quite the little cook all right." My father mimicked her use of the word little.

My family loved that word. It was a way to put me down with plausible deniability. They weren't being mean; it was simply a descriptor. At least, that's what they wanted others to perceive.

Otherwise, they came off as monsters. Cruel alphas and leaders of this pack.

Gods, I hated it here. If only I were brave enough to leave. But they'd hunt me down or, worse, they would hurt someone on my behalf. I was stuck here until they determined otherwise, and why would they? I did their bidding and showed the pack no one was immune to their power. I was invaluable to them—just, not in the way I wanted to be.

As the pack settled in with coffee and cupcakes, Lily manned coffee refills, and I started the dishes. There was *no room for a dishwasher* even though there was. Most nights, it wasn't too bad, but tonight, there were a ton, and the sooner I got started, the better the odds I'd get a few hours' sleep tonight.

"You forgot one."

I didn't turn around. It was Tyler. Once upon a time, when he thought I was going to be the next alpha, thanks to being born three minutes before my sister, he wooed me like I was a treasure. And my dumb ass? I believed he wanted me for me, that he thought I was special, that he might even love me. Not once did I suspect him to be my mate, but that was fine. I was going to be alpha. I didn't need a love match. I needed someone to rule by my side who didn't try to usurp my power.

"Leave it on the counter." I felt him come up behind me and add, "Please." I didn't get all the way through tonight to ruin everything by being rude to Tyler. I refused to give him that power over me.

"You know…" He scented me deeply, pressing his nose into the crook of my neck. His closeness caused my beast to press me for release. I had to force her down. Taking my fur in the kitchen would not end well. "I'm not opposed to you being a side piece—with discretion, obviously. Baby, we could be so good together. I remember the way you taste. I could never forget it."

I twirled around, attempting to get some distance between us, and the glass in my hand crashed to the floor and shattered into a thousand pieces. And as my father walked in, Tyler whispered, "There's no shame in it, kitten. No shame. We'll make sure you are well kept. If you don't, well, you might never see me again after tomorrow."

There wasn't even a second to ask him what that meant, my father calling for Lily to clean up my mess.

Chapter Two

Vargas

"Careful, Wilder." I laughed, walking up on a scene where my bond brother and best friend was bent down talking to the chickens like they were our children instead of egg-makers. "That's not really living up to our reputation."

He turned around, one chicken under each arm. That was his way. He treated our animals like his babies. That was why they were so healthy and thriving. "Gods, if we lived up to the whispers and daggers of others, I'd be drinking her blood or something. How was the honey harvest?"

Penn, our other bond mate, had taken most of this season's honey harvest to town, in glass jars with stickers on them that made sure no one knew where it came from. Otherwise, we wouldn't make a dime off it.

"It was good. We had tons to sell with enough to stock our pantry as well."

Wilder nodded and put the chickens down after a good talking to about fighting amongst themselves. I didn't know if it was the predator in him, but they seemed to listen, which was weird. "That's good. I'm done with chores. I'll see you later."

Wilder kept to himself a lot, but all of us knew where he spent his free time. One of the first things we'd done after we moved into the homestead was to make our future omega a nest. It was built into the room. It was a true nest, as far as we were concerned. A bedroom with an en suite. A giant bed in the middle. I had built the circular frame look like a bird's nest. We'd had the mattress custom made.

It had stood empty since then, but I was building a dresser for the room.

Not that we had an omega.

Or even a fucking chance in hell of ever courting one.

Not our pack.

"Have fun," I called and put my hands on my hips, looking out over our garden. The gods had blessed our season so far, and every day there were more things to pick.

I knelt on the ground and began pulling weeds. Snipping yellow crookneck squash from underneath their leaf umbrellas, I let out a breath. If I had my way, Wilder would give up on the pursuit of having an omega as I had years ago. Most packs courted and mated an omega early in life, as in their early twenties.

Then again, they weren't referred to as the bastard pack.

We were.

I worked in the garden for hours, plucking fresh produce and putting it all into baskets Penn would deal with after he came back from town. He was the brave one in that respect.

Town meant looks of derision and disapproval, and while we all could take it and were used to it, that didn't mean we volunteered for the meanness. That was why we chose our pack home here in the country, far away from prying eyes and the judgment.

I'd brought all the produce inside when I heard the *crunch* of truck tires on the gravel driveway. I didn't have to look through the window to know who it was. Penn was home and would have supplies with him that needed to be carried in.

We met him as he pulled in, but instead of getting to work, he emerged with a stern look on his face. Lines along his forehead. His shoulders tight.

"What happened?" I asked. Immediately, my thoughts went to the people in town, and I wondered if they'd heckled him. Damn it. I should've gone with him.

We knew better.

"Did something happen to the honey?" Wilder came from the side of the house. There were wood shavings on his T-shirt, and his collar and back were soaked with sweat.

"Nothing happened to the honey." Penn let that relief settle before he continued. "I heard something when I was in town. At the store."

We tried to be as self-reliant as we could, but there were things we couldn't produce on the farm. Flour. Sugar. Yeast. And I'd be damned if I was making my own pasta. Rice. The basics.

12

"What did you hear?" Wilder made his way to the back of the truck where he let down the tailgate and threw a few sacks of sugar over his shoulder.

"Put that down. Just listen. Please."

Whatever Penn had heard in town, it rattled him.

"Go on, then. Don't keep us in suspense." I fucking hated suspense. And surprises. Anything that came at me and my life out of left field.

"The Bronson pack has an omega."

Everyone had heard of the Bronson pack. They were powerful, and their offspring were always alpha, even the females. "The pack or the family?"

"The family. One of the twins. They were raised as alphas, but one of them presented as an omega when she turned eighteen."

Wilder shook his head. "And they're selling her? Like a plate lunch?"

Penn nodded. "The people who were talking…made it sound like they are trying to get rid of her."

"That can't be all that messed with you. What are you thinking, Penn?"

13

He nailed me with those intense eyes of his. "We don't really meet a lot of omegas out here. And most of them don't want us because…well because of who we are."

"You want to buy an omega?" Wilder asked.

"I want us to talk about it as a pack."

We all sighed.

"We need to do more than talk," I said. "Wilder, can you get on the computer and find out what you can on social media. I'm sure this rumor is hot in the shifter realm. Find out as much as you can. We need all the information before we even entertain this…idea."

The fact was, we all had the same idea without any of the discussion. Who we were didn't really have the omegas fighting over who could be ours. We didn't go to any of the social events intended to show off omegas to potential packs.

What we did have was money. We took care of our assets and saved like the apocalypse was on its way.

14

It sounded so barbaric, buying a mate, especially a precious omega, but it was the way of shifters around us.

"Good idea. I'll get on it as soon as we unpack."

We got everything inside, and Penn helped me process some of the vegetables for canning and dehydrating. We wasted nothing around here.

I cooked dinner while Penn went to his office. Wilder was in there as well.

I couldn't get too excited. Excitement gave us hope, and hope was not something we'd been able to afford before.

Chapter Three

Rumor

"Did we get everything?" I fisted the apron at my sides. Scanning the living room, I looked for anything out of place. Not because I gave a rat's ass about order and perfect neatness but because my parents did and would use anything, even a speck of dust, as a reason to tear me down even further. Much more of their correcting, and I'd be level with the ground.

I turned to see Lily fretting just as much as I was. Her cheeks were red as she cracked her knuckles. "I think so. Should we go over everything once again—"

Her sentence was cut off by my mother's footsteps coming down the stairs. My body froze, and everything inside me tightened in knots. "What are you two standing around for?" she asked. Gods, would it kill her to be my mother for once? I was only her daughter, it seemed, when I was good enough. Did enough. Worked myself to the bone enough. But even then, I was still an omega.

A shame to my family.

A leaf on the family tree they'd happily and easily blot out.

"We are making sure everything is perfect." I hated my tone when I spoke to her. It begged for approval. For a hint of love. The desperation for some kindness dripped from every word. *Please, please love me.*

"Perfect, huh? The food is prepared?"

She dropped to the last step and looked around. I checked off all the boxes in my head, knowing the triggers that would surely get me in shit with her. I saw none of them unchecked, but there was always room for a new one.

"Yes, Mother. Everything is ready."

"We'll see about that. We have some important people coming in tonight. Everything has to be perfect." She sidled up to me, but instead of feeling at ease as a daughter should, tingles broke out along my skin. Half of me wanted her to hug me. The other half wanted to step away from her evil. I knew she was ambitious about our pack and our family, but when I presented as an omega, it tore back all the layers of pretending and revealed the monster she was inside.

Lily nodded. "I'll go check on the preparations."

"There is one more thing that needs to be done. Let's go upstairs and get you ready." My mom grabbed my elbow and gave me little choice to do anything other than follow along.

Once in my bedroom, she pointed to a white dress that had a deep cut in the front and looked a size too small. It would've fit my lean and athletic sister Reyna just fine, but my curves had come in and there was no way that thing was fitting over my hips.

"What's this?" I asked, pointing to the slip of a thing.

"You have to look nice for the company tonight."

"Why?" The question dripped from my mouth, and I instantly wished I could retrieve it. We didn't question my mother. Rather, I didn't.

"Because we have to do something about your situation, Rumor."

"What situation?" Clearly, I was brave tonight.

"The situation where you are a shame to our family. The situation where only alphas are born in this family. Where the women are strong and capable." With each sentence, she got closer to me, her beady eyes digging in deep. "The situation where we need to get you...settled in a place where you can belong."

That last sentence cut me deep. I, as a person, wasn't up to their standards, therefore I didn't belong there. Was no longer pack. Was no longer family. I was something they needed to get settled somewhere else like an adopted puppy that chewed on one too many shoes.

"A place I can belong," I echoed.

"Don't make this harder than it has to be, Rumor. We are suffering too. It's hard for us to see you this way."

"It's not a disease," I murmured.

"It is to us. Bronsons don't give birth to omegas. We just don't. It's a stain on the otherwise clean and pristine cloth that is our family. Now, put on the dress. Let me see you in it."

There was no way I was subjecting myself to her sneers at seeing me undress in front of her. I ducked into the bathroom and put on the dress, tugging it so that all my parts were tucked into some covering.

I wasn't ashamed of my body, just didn't want to wave it around.

"I look like I'm for sale," I said, coming back into the room.

"Well, that's not far from the truth. We have alphas coming here tonight. In packs. We put the word out that a rare omega was on the market."

"The market?" I asked. Maybe if I smarted off enough, she'd hit me. Then I could have an excuse not to participate in whatever tonight was. Plus, hitting would hurt a lot less than the words she stabbed me with. "Like a pig or a cow at auction?"

My mother patted her hair and huffed a noise out through her nose. "Put it whatever way you will, Rumor. We can't have you here. Not in this family and not in this pack. Your sister is about to become our alpha, and we won't let anything bring her down. Tonight, you will mind your manners and be

21

respectful. Maybe you'll find a pack who can tolerate you. Find you attractive enough to bear children for them. Those hips were made for childbearing."

"Fine," I said. "Can you please go downstairs so I can fix my hair and get ready?"

She nodded and got up. "Fix that attitude while you're at it. This isn't easy for any of us. You're still on your suppressants? Make sure you wear plenty of scent blocker and those panties Lily got you."

It must be hard to sell your daughter off.

I was surprised she didn't clutch her pearls and cry.

I nodded, and she left quickly, but I didn't dare cry. As much as they wanted to get rid of me, I wanted to leave. I even had a few dollars put away in case I got a chance to flee.

I would probably get saddled with some old alphas or mean ones who might be crueler to me than my family. That would take some doing.

If I had daughters, I would leave. I would run for my life and theirs. They wouldn't endure this hatred, no matter who they were.

I pulled my hair down over my shoulder and slipped my feet into the shoes that matched my new awful dress.

"You can fucking do this, Rumor. This is your way out."

Chapter Four

Wilder

I polished off a third plate of Vargas' chicken with roasted cabbage and homemade garlic bread then waddled into the office and plopped into my office chair. Damn, he knew how to cook, but I felt like a tank after eating all of that.

Couldn't be helped. I was a growing boy.

I ignored all the notifications from Discord and my games begging me to play them and focused on the task at hand.

Time to find out more about the omega who was being sold.

Sold.

What a situation that we were even thinking about this.

I had set up social media accounts with names and profiles. We had to keep up with the shifter world somehow, and there were other packs like ours. The bastards had to stick together.

I checked everything I could find, which wasn't much. Names. Gossip. People talked, and shifters were the worst about coming up with a negative scenario when left to read between the lines.

There wasn't a single picture of this alpha turned omega. Born into a prominent pack of alphas as a twin, being an omega was even more rare. That had to be hard on the female. In an instant, because of something genetic the Goddess chose for her, she'd become the black sheep of the family, placed on the market.

For a high price. More than we'd paid for our land and the materials we used for construction of our house combined.

My wolf tugged at me through our connection. Even without a picture, a name, or much knowledge about the omega, he urged me to look further. Research more. Follow the segues.

And I did until there were no more left.

"Anything?" Penn stuck his head into our shared office.

"Yeah. I found some things. Get Vargas, please. Let's talk about this."

I waited and gathered my thoughts while Penn went off to find Vargas. We had a lot to talk over, but I would leave out the part where my wolf had already made his decision. If it were up to him, he would get in our Jeep and drive the fastest route to the Bronson pack to make our bid.

Why he was so attached all of a sudden was a mystery.

"I'm here," Vargas announced with Penn on his heels.

"Here's what I found out. It's not much. So, she's nineteen, almost twenty. She presented as an omega when she turned eighteen. She's a twin, and as we all know, twins are mostly both alphas, even females. She's basically being sold by the Bronson family because she's a black spot on their reputation of ruthless alphas."

Vargas snorted. "And yet, that's what they call us."

"No pictures?" Penn asked.

"Not a one. On the Bronson pack website, it looks like some pictures have been tampered with, so I'm

27

thinking they blotted her out altogether. But…do we care?"

"About what?"

"About her appearance. Think about it. She's been shunned from her family. Put on sale like cattle. Shoved out of her pack. Sound familiar?"

It did to me. Because our fathers bred out of their mating vows, we were rejected from shifter society. Our own pack. We took care of each other and the others who were like us.

Our fathers paid no price for their adultery.

But we paid everything.

So we took up the weapons they said we had. We built our reputation on things that would keep them away. Ruthlessness. Power. Meanness. Lawlessness. They made up the rest. We only started the fire.

"She's like us." Penn was right. She wasn't a bastard pup, but she was like us nonetheless.

"I hate this part of our society." Leave it to Vargas to say it out loud.

"We can use their indecency to our advantage," I offered. "She could be ours. We would treat her like our fated mate. We would be good to her when the rest of the world tried to bring her down."

Okay, that was a little sappy.

"How much?" Penn asked.

"Half of our savings," I said, showing him the screen that listed the purchase price for someone who should've been courted, not bid on. We alphas yearned to take care of an omega. Treat her like the queen that she was. Be slaves to her heat. Earn her love.

There were no objections.

"Who is going to go?" I asked. "If we all show up, it's going to look like an ambush."

We laughed. After the rumors we started and didn't refute, everyone thought we were the danger.

Not the fathers who abandoned us.

Vargas and I both looked at Penn. "What? Why me? I just went to town and peopled. That was bad enough. This is awful."

"But you're the least scary," I replied, cracking up.

"You're not scary, Wilder." Vargas shrugged. "That's me. You're not…as assertive."

"Asshole."

29

Vargas folded his arms over his chest. The man lived on good food and push-ups. And it showed. "And that assholery is why I'm not going. I already want to charge in there and give those people a piece of my mind. Selling off their daughter?"

Penn lowered his shoulders and blew out a breath. "Do they need cash?" He'd already accepted his fate.

"Doesn't say, but I haven't ever met a situation where it wasn't welcome." A truer statement had never been uttered. Cash was king.

"Do we have that much in the safe?"

I got up and punched in the combination and opened it. We had enough and more. Vargas didn't trust banks.

I didn't either.

We'd all received heavy inheritances from our fathers. Not because they were generous but as a buyout for us and our mothers to keep our mouths shut. We retained most of ours, since we'd bought the property at auction and built the house ourselves.

"When should I go?" Penn asked.

"Tonight," Vargas and I blurted at the same time.

"Eager, are we?" Penn said. "All right. Give me the address so I can plug it in, and wish me luck. I might just come back with our omega."

Chapter Five

Rumor

"Another one?" Lily whispered, holding my hands in hers. I was exhausted. Not from the physical exertion but because of the shedding of my self-respect. Little by little, I lost layers of it—watched it float to the ground and then disappear at the feet of the alphas who came in and then left.

In and out.

Coming and going.

I heard the door and thought, more like hoped, that it wasn't true. Through the afternoon and into the night, groups of alphas had come in. They were cordial, and their words were pretty, but none of them were owning-me material. Because when one chose me, that's what I would be—owned by them. Paid in full. Someone should write up a contract. *No refund. No returns. You break her, you buy her.*

"Rumor, come in here, darling."

Darling. What a fucking joke and insult. That woman had never muttered the word darling to me before. It oozed malice and insincerity. She'd better hope the alphas didn't catch on. Then again, they might not care. Most of them just wanted my labor and my uterus anyway.

I'd given up on love and fated mates a long time ago.

The day my fated mates chose my sister over me. All because I was an omega instead of an alpha. The Goddess must've needed a laugh.

"I'm here, Mother." I barely contained my portrayal of a prance, walking into the dining room. Oh, what fun it would be to dance into the room and curtsey. Goddess, they might like that.

"Here she is, Alpha Sharpclaw. Our omega. What a surprise she's been in our family."

Alpha Sharpclaw was as sharp as his namesake. One of his eyebrows cocked, and he smirked. "A surprise, huh? That's why there's such a large price on her head?"

My mother cleared her throat. I looked to my dad, hoping some of his alpha and fatherly instinct might kick in, but found disappointment in his blank stare.

"The price for her is minimal, I can assure you. She's primed for breeding. We come from a long line of strong, powerful alphas. Many of our family are alphas of their own packs. I have no doubt she will produce many sons for you."

Eew.

I shuddered with disgust. My mom was selling me as a breeder. I was born to lead this pack and have my own harem to support me, and this was where I landed? Shrunk down to a business proposition. An indecent one at that.

This was the same dialogue we'd had all day. Not the surprise part. That was a recent addition. Some of the alphas came in, took one look, and left. Others touched my hand and tried to flirt.

Alpha Sharpclaw soon joined the ranks of those who invaded my personal space, going so far as to lean in and scent my neck. That was the most personal thing a shifter could do, other than mating.

I really should grow a spine.

"She's on blockers. Heavy ones. I can't even get a scent," he said and stepped back. "I won't mate with an omega with little scent. How will we know when she is fertile?"

My mom looked at me, but this time I didn't falter. She was the one who wanted me on heavy scent blockers which included sprays, powders, deodorants, and panties. Everyone knew shifters chose mates by scent. Pheromones were important, even for humans.

"She is on blockers for her protection since she is unmated."

"Doesn't she want to find her fated mates?" He turned to me. Oh, goody, someone was going to speak to me directly for once. "Don't you wish for your fated mates?" My sister chose that moment to walk in with her mates, my former mates. I wanted to shrivel up, dig myself a hole, and bury myself there.

"I have no mates," I said, feeling some of that spine come in.

"Her mates chose to reject her."

The alpha shrugged and looked at me. Pity was all I saw in his eyes. "That's a shame. I will take my leave now. Thank you for your time."

As soon as he shut the door, my mother whirled on me. Her fists were balled, her cheeks red. She shook with rage. I scented it in the air like fire and charcoal. "Look what you did. Go upstairs and take that damned dress off. You never fail to shame me and our family."

I pulled my empty self up a few stairs. The worst part was, I was beginning to believe her words. Clearly, I was a shameful excuse for a female. No mates. Rejection. My sister stole everything from me. No one wanted me. I was an omega. I glanced over at Lily and saw the empathy in her eyes. Her life was my fate. I would end up cleaning the dirt of an alpha family's shoes. Rocking their children. Washing their dishes. My head down—where it should be.

I took a few steps but my wolf reared in my head. Something was pulling her down. Pulling me down with her. My feet became like concrete and every step was a struggle. I turned around to find the attention on me had quickly faded. My mother was gushing over

Reyna. My mates' eyes focused on my body. The mates Fate chose for me practically drooled over my curves in this strip of a dress. Maybe my wolf was pulling me to them.

A knock at the door stopped everything. The chatter. The movement. Even my breathing.

"Who is that?" My sister didn't even bother to say hello anymore. I was no longer her sister, her twin, despite the closeness we once shared.

My mother opened the door, and a man walked in. "My name is Pendleton. I came for the omega."

Chapter Six

Penn

The drive to the Bronson pack lands was over six hours away, but once we got on the road, I used the time to think, attempting to untangle the web we'd weaved ourselves into. We didn't even know her name; no one online mentioned it.

Glancing over to the passenger seat, I slid the brown envelope full of cash toward me. I had a vision in my head of the passenger door opening and the money floating away to the four winds. Silly, but it made me cautious.

My knuckles turned white as I gripped the steering wheel harder. I hated the ways of our kind sometimes. Buying females. Buying anyone for that matter. People weren't property or a commodity but at the very least, if this deal went through, we would consider the money well spent. This omega might not even be ours, but we could help free her from the cage she was in.

My highest hope? That she was our omega. That she belonged to us and us to her. That she was the one we'd been waiting and, personally, been praying to the Goddess for.

My wolf had a feeling that this trip would be life-changing. He made his presence known more than ever and as I drove the distance, he was right under the surface. Eager. Persistent. Ready.

I stayed in those lines of thought until I reached the gates of the pack.

"State your business." One of the pack members emerged from a makeshift security booth.

"My name is Pendleton Savage of the DarkShadow pack. I am here to visit the Bronson omega."

The pack members exchanged glances.

One of them nodded. "Go on, then. Straight to the alpha house. Go about your business and then leave as soon as possible. We don't want your kind here any longer than you have to be."

My kind. One mention of my name and all of a sudden, I was a different species or something.

I accepted his terms with a nod of my own and drove through the gates and to the huge house in the center. It screamed *a big, bad alpha lives here* or, to an outsider, someone who needs to prove their worth by building a mansion and using up so much of their pack's funds for showing off.

Throwing my truck into park, I steeled myself with a long sigh. I was moments away from potentially changing all of our lives.

All of us.

Money tucked under my arm, I got out and walked up the ginormous porch and knocked on the door.

A knot cinched up inside my stomach. Inside, I heard voices and then heavy footsteps.

"Who are you?" a younger man than I expected asked. Alpha and wolf by the scent of him. I thought the father would've opened the door—sized me up.

"My name is Pendleton. I came for the omega."

The man eyed the package under my arm and waved me inside. "Come in."

The house was filled with a group of men my age, all surrounding an alpha female. Then there was an older couple, the mother and the father, I assumed. The woman looked me up and down. "What pack are you from?"

"DarkShadow, ma'am."

One of the young men snickered, and the man who I thought was the father gripped the arms of his chair but didn't make a move to say anything or kick me out.

"This is our…this is Rumor. She is the omega I assume you're here for. I can't imagine you'd be here for any other business."

On the stairs was the embodiment of a curvaceous and stunning angel. She was dressed in a white, silky dress that did nothing to give her any kind of modesty. The way she had her arms crossed across her breasts and the way she bit her lip told me this wasn't her regular attire. She was uncomfortable, but her soft green eyes lifted to meet mine.

I attempted a smile to make her feel more at ease, but her mother's voice pierced the moment. "Rumor. Come down here. Let him get a good look at you."

Rumor stiffened her shoulders and walked down the few stairs on shaky legs. She had some high heels on that I also suspected weren't her regular attire. She oozed discomfort and anxiety.

When she came to stand in front of me, I was hit with her scent. Jasmine and vanilla punched me in the gut and sank every hang-up I'd had about coming here to get her.

She was ours. Pure and simple.

"He's from DarkShadow. You can't send her there," one of the men my age called out. The female they were with elbowed him in the ribs.

I ignored him.

"I'm Penn. It's lovely to meet you, Rumor."

"You too."

"Are you all packed up?"

Her eyes widened, and a smile lifted the corners of her lips. Either she was glad I was here, or she was simply that desperate to get the fuck out of here. I'd take her no matter which. "I am."

Her mother laughed. "We're getting a bit ahead of ourselves. As you know, our Rumor has a high price on her. She is an omega bred in a strong and powerful family."

43

I winked at Rumor and her cheeks bloomed with a rosy blush. "How about you go get ready to leave?"

Rumor turned and bolted up the stairs despite her mother's protests. "This is not the way we are doing this. You are not in charge here."

Nodding, I turned to the foul woman. "The money is here. In full. All cash. Please count it if you wish."

"You can't bring her back," the man in the chair grumbled.

"I would never return her here." Every bit of malice intended.

"How many are in your pack?"

"Three of us. All in good financial standing."

"Good. Evelyn, count the money. Make sure it's all there. Help her, Reyna. We all know the reputation of their so-called pack."

I handed over the brown paper bag. We had cushioned it with an extra thousand to test out the honor of these people. Although, since they were selling their daughter, we already knew. "Here you go."

"You are aware that she is an omega. Not the alphas we usually produce," the woman said, her hands full of cash and her eyes alight with greed.

"I do. What a treasure."

"A treasure," the other woman mocked. She looked to be the same age as Rumor, though with a completely different build and not half as beautiful. She must've been the alpha twin.

"Yes. Omegas are a gift from the Goddess."

"The money is all here," the older woman said to the older man. "I'll go make sure she's got everything ready." Her black eyes turned to me. "You're sure you want her."

"More than sure and I'm eager to get going back to our home."

They said nothing about the extra thousand. That fact spoke volumes.

Chapter Seven

Rumor

I bounded up the stairs as fast as I could. While this was my family, after the way they'd acted since I presented as an omega, I couldn't get out of here fast enough.

Mostly packed, I stuffed the last of my things inside the bag and changed into some jeans and a worn but soft and comfortable sweatshirt. My sister and I used to be clothed in the best of the best outfits but once I emerged as an omega, I could no longer wear anything scratchy or itchy or not the correct texture. Lily assured me it was all part of being an omega. After that, I turned to my more worn items plus the ones Lily gave me. Things she'd thrifted or handed down to me.

I frantically looked around the room with a new excitement in my step. The alpha who came for me, Pendleton, or Penn, looked kind. He had nice eyes, and his smile melted me instantly.

The sound of footsteps coming up the stairs made me freeze. Ugh. They'd done the deal—so why couldn't they leave me the hell alone?

"Rumor," my mother said, coming in. I busied myself with packing up last-minute things like my hairbrush and toothpaste.

"Yes, Mother?"

"The deal has been made. I see you are almost all ready to go, but we need to go over some things before you leave."

I stopped in my tracks and sat down to listen, but my eyes were darting around my room in case I missed anything. Like hell I would come back to get something even if I did.

"Tell me, please."

"Fine. Just know this isn't easy for any of us."

She was so full of shit, but the faster I got out of here, the better, so I kept my lips zipped and nodded.

"You are going to the DarkShadow pack to be their omega. Their mate. Their...well, whatever they deem you to be. They have paid the money."

"Okay."

My mother sighed. "You have to be sure to make the best of it. Do whatever they say because at the end of the day, you belong to them. After you leave tonight, you are no longer welcome in this house and are banished from this pack. Your sister will have a hard enough time with being a new alpha without extra problems."

"I understand."

"Do you? Because you either make it work with this pack or…"

I knew the *or*. Was best friends with the *or*. There was no going rogue for an omega like me. I would be recognized because of the pack I came from, and no good would come from my discovery.

When I first presented as an omega, I tried to kill myself. That night. Swallowed a bunch of wolfsbane and sat in the bathtub and welcomed my fate. That was the *or* my mother was referring to. When Lily discovered me and saved my life, my mother looked disappointed, not because I was alive but because I hadn't succeeded. Seemed I couldn't even take my own life properly.

Even more of a rejection in her book.

I squared off my shoulders and invoked my emotionless tone. "I understand what you are saying. I will go with Penn and the DarkShadow pack and never return here. I am no longer your daughter and will not contact you from this point further."

My mother got up and opened her arms. "One last hug?" she said.

"No."

I grabbed my bags and headed down the stairs. No looking back. No touching the banister to brand the memories in my head one last time.

The memories I once held dear had morphed into trauma the moment I wasn't what they wanted.

I was no longer their heir apparent. No longer their future alpha. No longer had my fated mates. I was nothing to them.

"Are you ready?" Penn asked, taking my bags from me.

"I am."

My father stood for the first time since Penn walked in. "This is her without all the hairdos and fancy dress. She's yours now. No refunds."

Penn nodded. "I understand. Let's go. Did you want to say goodbye to everyone?"

Then it dawned on me. I was going to be the omega of the DarkShadow pack. As the once future alpha of the Bronson pack, I knew their reputation. Ruthless bastards. Lawless rogues. Men without honor or a speck of kindness in their hearts.

"I...no. I don't."

"On the road, then. Follow me."

Penn put my bags in the back seat of his truck. He opened the door for me and once I was in the seat, he shut the door behind me.

Once inside, he paused. Oh, Goddess, was he rethinking this? Rethinking me? Already?

"What?" I asked. A knot built in my chest.

"Your seat belt. Won't move until you have it on."

"Oh." I scrambled to fasten it with shaking hands.

"Here. Let me." He was careful not to touch me while he brought it over my chest and secured it.

"There. It's a long drive. You must be tired. I brought a few blankets and a pillow if you'd like to rest."

"Thank you."

When we passed through the gates, the tears fell. Penn looked over, and I straightened and swiped them away with my wrists.

"Cry if you want to, female. I would be in pain as well."

I took him at his word and wept for at least an hour before passing out on the pillow he offered me. When I woke up, I was covered with a blanket and the cab was warm. The clock told me we were halfway through the trip.

Penn had pulled over at a gas station.

"I need to fill up. But first, let's get you something to eat."

"I...don't want to be any trouble."

He pursed his lips. They were full and supple-looking. I wondered if he would bother to kiss me with them before he and his pack ravaged me. "Feeding you when you're hungry is no trouble. Come on. Show me what you like. Anything you want."

We went into the dimly lit gas station. The attendant greeted us, and Penn kept a hand on my lower back while we walked. "I'm sorry I can't get you anything better. It's late at night, and this is the only thing open. They have sandwiches and chips."

I grabbed one of the chicken-salad sandwiches from the cooler and a small bag of chips and shrugged at him.

"Really? That's not enough for an ant, Rumor." My name on his lips warmed my chest. I'd been cold for so long. He proceeded to gather a pile of sandwiches, chips, snacks, and goodies and put them all on the counter. He smiled. Smug male.

When the attendant told us the total, I nearly fainted. "It's too much, but thank you."

"The boys would kill me if I brought you back starving."

"Would…would you tell me about your pack members?"

"Let me fill up the truck and then yes, absolutely." Penn filled up the truck and got in. "Why aren't you eating?"

"Oh. I was waiting for you."

He nodded. "No need for that. Dig in." We ate in record time, and I found myself yawning before I could get any more information about the pack I was destined to join. Or bought into.

As I fell asleep, I faintly noticed Penn brushing a strand of hair from my brow.

Chapter Eight

Vargas

No sleep was to be had until I saw Penn and our omega with my own eyes. We'd gotten a call from our packmate about an hour into their trip home. The deal was struck. The payment made.

Our omega secured.

We were betting everything on Penn's instincts. Everything. Our lives. Her life. Half of our life savings.

I didn't envy him the task, but now that he was in the truck with our female, the envy threatened to bubble over. He could see her. Scent her. Get to know her.

The person he carried home would not only be our omega, she would be our world, our mate, our partner, maybe the future mother of our children, though the last part was completely up to her.

"Vargas," Wilder called out. Sometimes Penn would call me Var but Wilder never did. He said Vargas was too short a name to make it even shorter.

I got out of bed and tugged on a hoodie, along with a pair of sweatpants that were hanging on a chair. Once in the hallway, I faced my friend, who was also pulling on a sweatshirt. He was thicker than the rest of us, but his heart was made of gold. He would give anyone the shirt off his back if they said the word. "What is it?"

"They're almost here. Penn texted me."

"He texted while our omega was in the car with him? That's dangerous. He's being reckless."

Wilder snorted. "What? He was probably at a stoplight. He would never endanger our mate."

It was strange to talk about a mate when we'd never seen her. Wonder about the future when we had never heard her voice or smelled her scent.

Good thing I had full faith in our packmate.

Or was trying to.

"Oh. Yeah. Of course. When are they…"

Wilder and I both stopped breathing and raised our heads a little. The *crunch* of Penn's truck tires on the gravel drive was undeniable.

He was back.

With our omega.

So I did what any mature alpha would do.

I shoved Wilder into my bedroom and made a run for it.

"Vargas. Godsdammt!"

He was on my heels in seconds, but we stopped short of the front door. "Okay. We have to calm down," I told Wilder whose chest was heaving from the sprint.

"Are you talking to me or yourself?"

I shrugged. "Both."

We made a show of taking a big breath and then opened the door. Penn was still driving up and soon parked in front of the cabin and turned off the lights. It was so black outside, even with my shifter sight, I couldn't see much.

Penn got out and my heart stopped. "She's asleep. Has been most of the drive." I nodded and barreled down the stairs alongside Wilder, but Penn stopped us. "She's scared and tired. She even cried in her sleep. It was heartbreaking."

"I'm not gonna eat her," I barked. "You don't need to protect her from me."

"Or me," Wilder echoed.

"I know that, but she doesn't. She doesn't know us. Only our reputations. We have to take things slow."

Wilder put his hand on my arm. "Let's go and sit on the porch. We'll let Penn wake her up since she knows him. The last thing we want to do is bombard her."

He was right but damn it all, I wanted to see her. My wolf was outright feral inside me. He knew she was ours. No name. No scent. No face-to-face meeting.

"Fine."

Penn nodded and went to the passenger door while Wilder and I sat on the steps. I sat on my hands, knowing otherwise, I would wring them with anticipation.

My heart was ready to burst from my sternum.

I heard a sweet ting of a voice and Penn pulled the blanket from her. "I can carry you," he offered.

"It's okay. I can walk. But thank you."

Her voice wrapped around my torso and squeezed. My wolf went ballistic.

Go to her. Go to our mate. Carry her. Bring her to her nest.

She got out and looked to the porch. Wilder's knee bobbed. My breath caught in my throat.

Forget the Goddess that created our kind, she was a Goddess in her own right.

"Her name is Rumor," Wilder said. Shit, had I said that Goddess bit out loud?

Her blonde hair flowed in rivers down each shoulder and across her ample chest. Once the door was closed, I could see her curvy hips and hourglass figure. The worn-out clothes she wore somehow didn't detract from her beauty one ounce. She walked over and stayed one step behind Penn. Of course she did. He was all she knew of protection, and he was her ticket to freedom.

Wilder and I stood as she got closer.

"Rumor, this is Wilder and this is Vargas. This is your…this is our pack."

Wilder smiled and went down the stairs. "It's nice to meet you, Rumor."

She looked at me with those minty-green eyes. My words lodged in my throat like a boulder. "Rumor, it is lovely to meet you," I choked out. "Welcome to our home. Your home."

She nodded and a few things happened at once.

One, I was hit with her scent. Vanilla and jasmine and everything sunshine in this world.

Two, she stepped back, blushing, with her hand on her chest. "I'm sorry."

"Sorry?" I asked. "Whatever for?"

"My blockers only last so long. It's...my scent. I'm sorry."

Wilder stepped closer but she didn't budge. "Your scent is beautiful, omega. There's nothing to be sorry for."

"Your scents are...this place... Oh..." Penn and I both reached out as her knees buckled.

I caught her up in my hold, honeymoon style, and turned to my brothers. "Penn, can you grab her things? Wilder? Her nest is ready?"

Wilder nodded. "I washed everything this morning and made it all up."

"I'm putting her to bed."

I carried our omega, sweet and scared as she was, up the stairs where we'd built her nest. Hers was the only room upstairs and she had the floor to herself. One day, she might invite us to join her there. Maybe in her heat. Or simply for her comfort, but until then, it was hers. It had always been hers.

I brought her to the round, built-in bed and laid her across the soft comforter. We'd shopped all the omega outlets to find the best comforters and blankets for her nest. The plushiest pillows. The best of the best even though at the time, we didn't have a whisper of her. If she took to us, accepted our courting and us as a pack, she would probably start stealing some of our shirts and clothing that smelled like us. I'd walk around naked if she wanted everything I owned. We'd waited so long for her.

I could only hope she let us be hers.

"There you go, sweetheart," I whispered. "Rest well."

Penn came up with her bags and helped me pull off her shoes and tuck her in. Wilder cracked the windows a bit. He said he hoped the sounds of the wild would comfort her.

It was dawn before we closed the door to her suite and I could finally breathe again.

Chapter Nine

Rumor

I never wanted to get up from this bed. Ever. My feet rubbed against the soft sheets surrounding me. Too bad I had jeans on. And a sweatshirt.

Huh?

Reaching up, I peeled the luxurious blanket from the side of my face and was hit with streams of sunlight pouring into the room.

Oh, Goddess.

I sat up in a flash and scanned the room. The events of the night before came flooding back to me. The completion of the sale. Packing up. Leaving. Riding in the truck. Crying. The cab of the truck filled with Penn's scent.

And then when I arrived…oh, those alphas. Penn was handsome in his own way, and I thought maybe the other two hadn't come because they weren't somehow. The silly things we make up in our heads.

But once I saw them, Wilder and Vargas, well, I knew the depths of my ridiculousness.

All three of them were breathtakingly attractive and sexy.

I said hello to them, but their scents overwhelmed me. Their scents. The night. The trauma of leaving my home, the only home that I'd ever known. The disgust I had for my parents.

I'd forgotten to say goodbye to Lily one last time.

I faintly remembered someone touching my face and whispering something to me before I completely dived into the pool of the deepest sleep I had ever had.

Wait a damned minute. The sun was up. It had almost been up by the time Penn and I got back to the house, but now? It was very much morning, and I wasn't pulling my weight. That was a line directly from my sister's mouth.

First day, and I was failing. Shit!

I found that my room had an adjoining bathroom, and I rushed through a shower and brushing my teeth before finding another pair of jeans and a T-shirt that had seen better days but was comfortable and soft against my skin.

Padding down the stairs, I tried not to make any noise. I knew next to nothing about the pack I was now living with. Did they work from home? Were they even home, or had they gone somewhere? Heck, I was looking for a kitchen and I had no idea where.

Luckily, the kitchen was to the left of the bottom of the stairs. I saw no one else around and my wolf didn't sense any movement. I hoped my arrival hadn't thrown off their schedules or work. I couldn't afford any mistakes…at least, not yet.

With cabinets open and a large pantry as well, I familiarized myself with the layout before starting. In only a few hours, I'd baked two large loaves of bread and they were cooling on racks. I'd made a dozen scrambled eggs. Roasted potato wedges. Cooked up pork sausage links that claimed they were locally sourced and processed. I'd just finished off the fruit salad when I heard a noise.

Someone was coming down the stairs.

More than one someone.

"Rumor?" someone said. It wasn't Penn. I knew his voice well.

"I'm here."

All three of them came down the stairs. Vargas and Penn only had shorts on, but Wilder wore a white T-shirt with jeans. All of them barefoot. Messy hair. Sleepy eyes. I sighed. With looks like that, why in the world had they come after me?

"Good morning," Penn said and came over to the island where I'd put all the food.

"Good morning. All of you."

Vargas, the one with the darker hair came over to me. I froze, not knowing what he might do, but he pushed a strand of hair from my face. Oh. Now that made sense. He was the one who must've done it the night before. "What have you been into this morning? You did all of this for us?"

I nodded. "Yes," I said. I left out the part where I knew that's what omegas did and they shouldn't be so surprised.

"Thank you, Rumor. This is incredible. You didn't have to."

"Oh." I looked out over the offerings. Sure, I'd gone overboard, but it was nothing out of the ordinary.

Vargas and Penn excused themselves and came back only a few minutes later wearing clothes more like Wilder. They showed me how to prepare the coffeepot, and I internally beat myself up for not thinking about coffee.

Coffee.

A staple for anyone. I didn't drink it myself. My mother said it made me feisty. She didn't like feisty, except in the case of an alpha. Then it would've been acceptable.

"I'm sorry," I muttered, expecting a dressing down for the blunder.

All three of them stared at me as though I'd turned into an aardvark.

Penn walked over and put his hand on my arm but quickly removed it. "Why?"

"I forgot to make the coffee?"

Wilder turned around from the cabinet where he was pulling a jar of honey down. "Rumor, everyone in this house is perfectly capable of brewing coffee. If one of us doesn't, another will. There's nothing to apologize for."

Huh. "Okay."

We worked together, taking out plates and silverware and placing all the food on the table before everyone sat down. I was offered coffee by more than one of the packmates, but I declined.

The last thing I needed was to be feisty.

"Everything smells incredible, Rumor. Thank you for this. Really."

They said that, but none of them had moved to fill their plate. Was something wrong? Had I missed a step or fumbled over some manners?"

One way to find out. "You're welcome, but why aren't you eating?"

Vargas smiled at me. He had warm eyes. Inviting even. "We are waiting for you to eat, omega. In this house, alphas eat last. Would you like me to make one for you?"

"I don't understand."

"Which part?" Penn asked.

Chapter Ten

Wilder

"Which part?" Penn asked Rumor as she sat, wide-eyed. Her posture had shrunk back a bit as we sat around the table.

At first, when we walked down, she seemed torn and now, it was like she was turning invisible by the second. Had we done something to offend her?

"I don't understand why you would wait for me to get a plate. Omegas eat last, and not with the family." She jerked from the table as though it burned her. "I shouldn't even be sitting here. I've forgotten my place. I'm sorry." She stood and turned away. "I need to start cleaning up my mess."

Not on my watch. I rose before she could take a step, and grabbed her by the waist. She gasped as I picked her up and sat her back down in the chair. "That's not the way we work."

"I-I don't…"

Understand, I finished for her in my head.

I reached out for the hand closest to me, and she didn't pull away. "Rumor, please listen to us. One day, you'll be able to tell us what happened at your parents' home and under their care, but for right now, we need to let you know how our home will be run now that you are here."

A tear slipped from one of her eyes, and she was shaking. Was she scared of us? Either way, the sight of this beautiful female crying stopped any further words from escaping my mouth.

I looked to Vargas, who nodded and said, "We value omegas here, Rumor."

Her natural perfuming grew sharp in my nose.

"Only one omega, right?" Penn said, correcting Vargas's slip of the tongue.

"Of course. You, Rumor. You're the only omega who has ever been here." The only one who would ever be, as far as I was concerned, and I was sure my bond brothers felt the same. The scent of attraction and lust bloomed in the air as soon as she arrived. Vargas continued, "Where we come from, omegas eat first. They are special and revered. Good alphas make sure

their omega is well taken care of, and that starts right
now with breakfast."

"You…" Her voice shook. Gods, what had they
done to her? "You want me to eat with you? Only pack
eats together."

The brainwashing ran deep. Wherever Rumor had
gotten her information about omegas and how packs
work, well, I wanted to line them up and give them a
piece of my mind and my fists.

"You are a member of this household now," I
assured her. "We are a pack and you are now a
member of this pack. Not officially yet, but you have
all the rights and privileges we all do."

"You want me in this pack?" Her green eyes
flicked to mine, searching for confirmation. At least
she knew I would tell her the truth.

I nodded in response.

Penn took her other hand and like me, she let him.
"Always, omega. We want to spend as much time as
possible with you. So let's all eat. I'm going to put a
little of everything on your plate. You eat what you

like and as much as you want and let us know what you don't."

"Don't you like coffee, Rumor?" Vargas asked.

"I wasn't allowed coffee," she whispered.

There were necessities in this life. Death. Taxes. And coffee. She was clearly missing a big piece.

"I'm getting you a cup. What do you like in it?"

She faintly smiled. "Ungodly amounts of flavored creamer, please."

"You got it." Vargas poured her a cup, humming. He placed it in front of her. As she took her first sip, she let out a noise of approval, and I tensed. Gods, I hoped I could find a way to coax that sound out of her in the future. If by no other means than more coffee.

We began to eat but only after she took her first bite. We were gentlemen, after all.

"So, how did you sleep, Rumor?" I asked after watching her down half the plate. I saw her eyeing more toast and I took the liberty of putting some on her plate.

"Like the dead, actually. It's…it's been a long time since I slept that well. Did you put me in someone's room? Is that the place I'm going to be staying?"

I swallowed. Of course it was. That was the room and the nest we put together with only the dream of her in our minds.

"It's your room," I said plainly. "It's all yours."

"Oh. It's beautiful. Thank you. The bed is incredible. I've never seen a round bed before."

"Wilder custom built it."

If I wasn't melted before, I was a puddle now. I would give her anything she wanted—anything that I had to give. "You did? It's really something."

"You don't like cantaloupe?" Penn asked, noticing the pile of the orange fruit on the side of her plate."

She wrinkled her nose. "I really don't. It tastes…musky."

Note taken.

"No more cantaloupe growing for you, Vargas," I laughed. "Well, maybe only to sell."

"You grow these?" she asked.

"We grew all the fruit on this table. And we gathered the honey in that jar. We make the preserves in those jars from the fruit on our trees. The eggs come from our chickens out back."

"Right here?" She looked around.

"Right here," Penn offered. "How about we finish up and take a tour around our farm?"

Her face brightened. "I would like that. Thank you. But…" Her gaze drifted to the kitchen. It wasn't a bigger mess than any of us would have made.

Vargas stood. "I've got cleanup duty this morning. We all take turns, okay?"

She tugged at a few blonde hairs floating in front of her ear. Was it as silky and smooth as it looked? "Okay."

Penn and I walked around with her while Vargas stayed behind to clean up. She seemed in awe of the whole place. She asked questions about what was growing and stood slightly behind Penn as we showed her the bees. The chickens flocked to her like a magnet, and so did Old Bay, our German shepherd. He mostly stayed outside, by choice, but I had a feeling he would come in more often now. Even the sunflowers seemed to turn in her direction.

74

"We sell a lot of our produce and honey in town, but we preserve and eat most of it. We also have a freeze dryer and a dehydrator. We have become pretty self-sufficient over time."

Vargas walked up behind her as we stood there. "You won't ever want for anything here."

She jumped a mile high and clutched her shirt at her chest. Her clothes were worn and her jeans were too big for her.

"Sorry. I didn't mean to scare you."

"It's okay." Her breaths were ragged. "I'm a little on edge. Everything is new."

We walked around the place some more, Old Bay at Rumor's side the entire time. When we got to the back door, she paused and whirled around to face us. "Is there something I can do to contribute? You all have your niches here. I would like to be a part of that if that's possible. I don't want to step on any toes."

Vargas put his hand on her shoulder. "You would never be stepping on any toes, omega. I'm sure you have talents you are yet to discover."

Chapter Eleven

Vargas

It was Rumor's first day here, and as much as I wanted to spend every waking moment with her, she needed space and time. A lot happened to her all at once. When I discovered that she hadn't even known about the alphas coming last night until just beforehand, my wolf tried to tear through me and go and hunt her family down.

No.

Not her family. The people she was blood related to. We were her family now, and we would protect her with our lives, especially from them. It had been all I could do to keep him in check. If I hadn't pressed upon him that shifting in anger would scare her, I doubt I'd have been able to control him.

When Rumor asked what she should do today, it was obvious she meant chores. All three of us were in agreement, she needed to take time to adjust to her new pack, to rest, to explore the property. I had to admit that I thought that would be easier for her than it was. She hadn't been allowed even a second's rest in so long that taking a break had her fear responses kicking in.

I fucking hated her family.

When Penn came to us with the idea of rescuing her—because I refused to think of her as a purchase— his gut had told them her life had been bad. They rejected her as soon as she presented as omega and then treated her absolutely horribly. Far worse than I could've imagined, and I didn't even know all of it. Between what little she told us and what Pendleton had witnessed, I didn't need all the details to know it was a position I'd never wish upon my worst enemies.

Poor, sweet Rumor had been treated like trash and then sold to the highest bidder. I still felt awful—that we purchased her. It wasn't something I'd ever feel comfortable with. But if buying her freedom was the only way for her to have it, then that's what we had to do. We didn't have the strength or numbers to start a war with them. And even if we did, it would put her at risk. I refused to ever do that.

It was a horrible system, but it was the one we had to work with.

My patch of carrots needed weeding and I had vegetables to harvest for dinner, so I went outside—hating that I was leaving her, but also knowing she probably needed a little space. Going from no positive attention to positive attention from three had to be overwhelming.

It had been a gorgeous morning, but I could feel that things were about to change. The sky was an odd color and the air was too still. A storm was coming, and I changed what I planned for dinner to a stew, because there was nothing better than stew on a rainy evening.

I brought the veggies I harvested into the kitchen and cleaned and chopped them, getting ready to assemble dinner. I loved cooking. Something about taking the things that I grew and turning them into nourishing meals for my pack was so satisfying.

Not just about nutrition and making them smile with delicious food—mealtime was important to us. It was when we got together, shared our day, made plans, and enjoyed each other's company. For a long time, it had been three of us. Now it was four.

Rumor had been wandering around, peeking in the kitchen, pulling back and repeating. She was hovering, and I wasn't sure why. I pretended not to notice for a while in an attempt to not make her feel uncomfortable. But, eventually, my wolf couldn't handle it anymore. Her scent was teasing him, calling to him, but he also wanted to comfort her.

"Rumor, why don't you come in? You can sit at the counter and talk to me while I'm cooking."

"I can help—peel carrots." She was so quick to try and help. If I thought it was simply out of desire to do so, I'd take her up on it. But until she learned and believed that we didn't expect her to be our servant, I had to be cautious not to let her overdo it.

"I've got it. Just keep me company."

"Are you sure that's enough?"

That was everything.

"Yeah, I'm sure."

She walked over. Even if I didn't know her and how kind she was—even if I hadn't smelled her jasmine-vanilla perfume, she'd have taken my breath away. She was absolutely stunning, and I didn't think she had any idea how gorgeous she was. Wilder, Penn, and I were going to need to fix that.

Even in her worn, torn, ill-fitted clothing, she had all of my attention. Not even a potato sack could hide those delicious curves.

We needed to buy her some clothes that showed her personality, didn't have holes in them, and she didn't have to pull up or pull down because they were either too tight or too loose. It was going to be fun taking her out and spoiling her.

"I used to do the cooking," she said, picking at her fingernail, her leg bouncing enough that I could feel the slight tremor against the counter.

"Did you like it?"

She looked up at me like I asked her something shocking, instead of just a simple preference.

"It was what I did." Which wasn't a yes.

"I love cooking. It makes me happy to put food on the table that everyone enjoys."

She gave me a small smile, and I wanted to capture it for always. We needed to make sure she had plenty of reasons to reward us with her smile.

"Tell me something you do like." We knew so little about her beyond her circumstances.

She half shrugged.

"You said, before you were eighteen, everybody thought you were an alpha. What did you do then?"

I didn't want to say "before they made you their slave," which was pretty much what they'd done to her.

"I like to read." She squished her lips to the side as if she was thinking really hard about it. "I like to paint, but not like pictures. I like to paint furniture, and I really like to paint rocks."

"Rocks?" What a fascinating omega our mate was.

"Yeah. I like to see what they look like. Have you ever laid on the grass and watched the clouds and you saw what they were meant to be, like a rabbit or a dragon or a train?" It was evident that she hadn't talked to a lot of people about this, the way she stammered to find the words. But she was sharing it with me…she

82

saw me as worthy of seeing this side of her. My wolf was front and center, already so in love with our mate.

"I still do that," I confessed and her smile grew.

"I do that with rocks—see what they're meant to be, and then paint them so that they look like that item. Is that weird?"

"No, that's absolutely wonderful. We have a lot of rocks we removed from the soil when we expanded the garden. Maybe I can show you after dinner."

"I'd like that."

I'd talk to the guys about getting her some supplies. If painting made her happy, then we were going to make sure she had access to what she needed to do so.

"And you said you like to paint furniture too. Do you mean like so it's pretty, or to refinish it?"

She went on talking about how she liked to connect pieces in a room that didn't necessarily go together through little details in her paint work. It was fascinating and, for the first time, I felt like I got a glimpse of Rumor, unfiltered.

My mate was full of surprises.

83

Our mate was full of surprises.

I popped the lid on the stew. It was at the set-it-and-forget-it time—and started working on the dishes. When she offered to dry, I let her. I didn't want her to think we were rejecting her offers for always and forever, but also, I didn't want her to feel like she had to do everything. This felt like a good compromise.

We had just finished up when the others came in.

"It smells so good." Wilder stepped inside first.

"Thank you. It's just stew."

"Oh, the stew. Yeah, that too." He winked. He was right, though, our mate's perfume was mesmerizing.

"Oh, Wilder..." She snapped her mouth shut, her cheeks a rosy pink. There was no fear coming off of her. She liked that he appreciated her scent.

"I'm gonna set the table," Penn said.

Penn grabbed the drinks while I brought the stew and rolls over. Minutes later, we were at the table eating, none of us taking a bite until our mate did.

I could see the awkward discomfort on her face as she took the first one, but the three of us alphas had talked about it and decided this was the best way. It was important for her to embrace her new role here, one that was not of someone lesser than the others. And if these first couple days of her being unsure meant a lifetime of happiness, contentment, and ease, then it was worth it.

Wilder leaned closer to Rumor and sniffed. "You smell different today. Rumor, are you maybe going into heat?"

Rumor looked like she wanted to melt into the floor and disappear. Wilder hadn't meant it to be rude, but intentions didn't matter…not when our mate was hurting.

"My mother made sure I stayed on my suppressants." Her answer was cold and practiced. I hated it.

"Oh—I wasn't trying to be… I just...you didn't smell like you. There was no jasmine and vanilla. I like those." He wasn't helping.

"It's scented suppressant," she mumbled.

Penn gasped. "Why do you use that?"

"Because I'm supposed to. I have to."

We were walking a very fine line here. We didn't want to scare her or make her feel like we were invading her space, but also, she needed to know how categorically unlike her family we were.

"Rumor, if you like those sprays, use them. But don't use them for us." If I had my way, she'd never use them again, but it wasn't up to me.

"You don't need to use any suppressants, if you don't want to. We'd gladly help you through your heat, or we could just keep you safe while you handle it on your own." Wilder put his fork down. "But you don't need all of that unless it's what you want."

"You would…my... I'm…I'm suddenly not feeling well."

She put her napkin down and ran off.

Fuck.

Chapter Twelve

Rumor

Wilder hadn't mean anything by what he said. None of them had. They'd been nothing but amazing to me at every corner.

But hearing the mention of my heat, my suppressants, my scent blockers—it was all too much.

I was too visible.

Too seen.

I wasn't hiding or blending like I needed to. No. Not what I'd grown to believe was needed. I'd been forced to be invisible, ever since coming out as an omega. I had my place and it wasn't with the alphas.

And now I was in the bathroom crying…because that helped.

"Come on, Rumor. Pull it together." I grabbed a washcloth and ran it under cold water. I held it to my face, willing the tears back, hoping I wouldn't look every bit the mess that I was.

These alphas were different. They were. And they weren't saying, "Oh, I'm different. You can trust me." I'd met alphas like that before. Wilder, Penn, and Vargas showed me they were different.

They let me eat first. They might never understand how meaningful that small gesture was. It would be a while before it would be automatic for me, but I was getting there.

They didn't throw chores at me. They barely let me help. That wouldn't last forever. I liked being useful but being a choice...wow.

The first time I saw Penn, I knew he'd be kind to me, and that he was a better option than staying where I was. I had no idea about the others, but it hadn't mattered because the bar had been in the basement, so it had already been surpassed simply by him giving me that small smile.

This should be easy. I was someplace where people actually wanted me. Adjusting shouldn't be difficult, except it was. There was so much to take in.

I pulled the washcloth from my face and peered in the mirror to make sure I didn't look too much of a mess. I very much did. Anyone would know I had been crying. I pulled my hair forward to try to shade my face a little, braced myself, and walked out. These alphas, my mates, deserved better than me melting down and hiding from them simply because I was freaked out over a sex talk that hadn't even included sex really, just the mention of heat.

I don't know why I was surprised to find Wilder standing there, arms open. I shouldn't have been. His face had fallen when he realized what he'd said. He wasn't being a dick, just comfortable enough with me to say all the things.

"Hey, I just wanted to—"

I threw my arms around him at the invitation of his open ones and clung to him for dear life as he held me, so gently, so sweetly.

When was the last time I'd been hugged?

Never, since I was an omega.

But before that, when I was an alpha? Alphas didn't need affection. They needed to be strong. Tough. To do things on their own.

Try as I might, a memory of being hugged anytime after I was very small didn't come to me.

But here I was. Wilder, holding me close, telling me he was sorry. I was the one who should be apologizing. I was the one who ran out, too weak to deal with a reasonable conversation. But when I tried, he asked me not to, to let him bear it.

"I'm ready to go back in." I pulled back and wiped my tears with my hands, no longer worried about what I looked like, feeling so accepted by him.

He apologized again.

"Please don't apologize," I said. "Wilder, I-I overreacted. You didn't—"

His hand came up and cupped my cheek, and I leaned in to his touch. "You didn't overreact. You've been through so much more than I'll ever know, and I was insensitive. If you don't want to come back to dinner, we'll understand. I can bring you food to your room."

"I want to," I said, and I started walking that way because if I thought about it too long, I probably would go and hide in my nest. The one they made just for me.

90

The one place they promised never to enter without my permission. I'd never had that before. I was always either in my parents' house or the omega house.

My new pack was nothing like the old.

I sat down and thought to apologize again but bit it back. I didn't want them to see me this weak. But I did want them to see me, something I hadn't realized before.

They must have sensed I didn't want to rehash my distress from earlier, because the first thing Vargas did was tell me that he'd just been talking to Wilder about my rocks.

"I was always told it was a silly hobby," I said, "but you guys seem interested."

"We're interested in everything about you," Penn stated very matter-of-factly. "Now, this is new to us. We've never had an omega in our pack before, and we want to do right by you. We want you to feel this place is every bit as much yours as it is ours. And that we're making your days better—not harder."

"I can't believe you guys want me here." I hadn't meant to say it aloud, but out it came.

"Why wouldn't we? You're amazing." The sincerity in Wilder's words floored me. It was very clear he didn't have the best filter, but that gave such a sense of honesty to the words he did share.

"Because I've been rejected," I admitted.

And it was true.

They rejected me.

I was sloppy seconds.

An outcast.

First, I was rejected by my family, then rejected by my mates, then by most of the alphas wanting to buy an omega. Nobody wanted me.

Until Penn.

"The best thing that's ever happened is them rejecting you," Penn said, "because we hadn't found you yet."

Penn reached over to touch my hand but pulled back. They were still so nervous around me. But then again—I was nervous around them too.

"You're so brave and strong," Vargas said.

Wrong.

I scooped some more stew onto my plate, not even asking, something entirely new to me. Maybe I was brave or getting braver.

They had to have noticed I left all the carrots. They weren't my favorite. I'd eat them eventually—or maybe not. I suspected that they wouldn't care if I chose not to eat things because they weren't my preference.

That hadn't always been the case for me. It was, *eat everything or don't eat the next meal*, even before they knew I was an omega. It had always been about power and control.

"I'm not strong. Trust me, I'm not."

"Of course you are. You came to us. You came to the bastard pack. That's the kind of brave most people won't even consider."

I didn't have the heart to tell them that my choices were to trust them—or end my life and be with the Goddess. Because one thing was for sure. I wouldn't have stayed there. That life had been no life at all.

Chapter Thirteen

Penn

I tended to be the one to go to town to run the errands. I didn't mind going to the market or peopling as much as the others did, and it had sort of become my task. But this week was different.

Rumor had been with us for a while now and seemed to be settled in at home—comfortable enough that we wanted not only to show her town but help her pick out some things to make her life easier.

What she brought with her was sad and borderline ragged, so I'd attempted to find her some things she might like. Picking out clothes for a woman had turned out to be much more difficult than I thought it would be. The few things I brought back for her were either for people far taller or were impractical in ways I hadn't considered—making it difficult for her to do the things she loved while wearing them. She never said anything other than "thank you," and how much she appreciated them, but I could tell. She even wore the formal skirt I'd brought, one I hadn't realized was so formal and restrictive, around the house.

Time for her to choose items she loved.

Of course, as soon as Rumor agreed to come, Wilder and Vargas wanted to come as well. None of us liked being far from her, and our wolves…they were especially protective like that. Being off pack lands without us wasn't going to happen.

Unless she said it was what she wanted. We'd promised her she wasn't our property, she had full freedom, and we would honor that, even if it meant she chose not to be our mate.

We needed a lot of farm things—chicken feed, seeds, bulbs for the flower garden Rumor planned. And, of course, anything else Rumor desired. If her eyes lingered on anything for more than a few seconds, I was making sure she got it. The first place we headed was the farmer's market.

It was a nice day, and, as we walked around, Rumor got more and more relaxed—more and more comfortable with the visit. She found a couple of aprons she said would be good smocks for the painting she'd been doing. Of course, we picked up plenty of soaps from the goat farmer. I was happy to see that she picked one with a light scent, given how when she arrived, she did everything she could to block her own. It felt like a big step.

At the far end, there were baby chicks, which were always adorable, as well as baby bunnies.

"Look! They have quail!" Rumor rushed over and squatted to get a better look. "I love quail eggs. I haven't had one in… It's been a while."

She didn't talk about her family, but once in a while, little things would slip out, some boldly and others like this, reminding us her parents stopped giving her the good food at presentation. They really did suck.

"Is that something you'd like?" I asked. "Because we could raise some quail."

"Really?"

"Of course. Right, guys?"

The others nodded.

"But maybe we'll start with the chicks and not start with hatching eggs," I added. I wasn't opposed, but we didn't have an incubator or everything set up. Felt a little risky.

Varga and Wilder went off to get supplies for the new coop. We needed to keep them separate from the chickens, at least initially. Vargas was the builder and Wilder the animal guy, so it made sense I was the one who stayed behind.

I helped Rumor pick out which quail we'd take home, and while they were being boxed up, we hit up the bakery table.

We always had pretty good eats at our house, including baked goods, but there was something magical about the cookies at this particular stand. We stocked up fairly often, putting them in the freezer for whenever we wanted them. Today was no exception.

But just as Rumor was reaching for one of the boxes, she froze. Something was wrong.

I turned around and saw her sister standing behind me. If I had even suspected she was there, we'd have already been on our way home. The last person our mate needed to come in contact with on her first outing to town was a member of her family. Fuck, she didn't need that any day.

I brought my lips low and close to Rumor's ear, whispering only for her, "Let's go back to the truck."

She grabbed my hand, held it tight, and we wove through the crowd. As far as I could tell, Reyna hadn't seen us—which was good. Because if we had words... Oh, was I going to have some choice ones.

I helped Rumor into the truck. She didn't even stop long enough to greet her mates. That's how shaken up she was. The guys were already there, having just finished loading the coop supplies.

"We need to go back for the quail," I said. "Vargas, stay with her."

I didn't say why, but he agreed without question. His wolf was so close to the surface, I could see him in his eyes. It was best he wasn't around people other than pack right now.

Wilder and I worked our way back, and, as we passed Reyna, she snarled at us and said, "If you try and return her, we aren't giving you shit back. We wouldn't even take her back. She's dead to us."

I growled.

I fucking growled.

I didn't care who heard me—human or not. She stumbled back. Good. Fuck her.

Wilder and I grabbed the quail and rushed back to our mate. We both agreed, her seeing Reyna again was not a good idea.

On the way home, Rumor was quiet. Silent, even. We didn't push.

But something changed when we arrived on our pack lands. As if I could feel her relaxing.

"I didn't think she could hurt me anymore," she mumbled.

"She's always going to…"

Chapter Fourteen

Rumor

I hadn't expected to see Reyna again. Ever.

I preferred it that way.

But when I heard her voice, my blood ran cold. She was there at the same farmer's market as me.

Why?

It wasn't the type of place she tended to go. It wasn't fancy enough; it was too dirty, too beneath her. There was absolutely no reason for her to be there. Was it to find me?

Probably not. She didn't have a reason to hunt me down, right? She didn't even try to talk to me. It had to be a crappy coincidence.

And really, I didn't care what her reason for being there was. It didn't matter. I wasn't going back to that market. I couldn't risk it. Not again.

I only got a glimpse of her. I don't know why I assumed she was going to be pregnant already, but it caught me off guard to see her there, looking no different than always.

Why the fuck was I thinking about that? Or her at all. She had nothing to do with me anymore. And I couldn't let her in my head like that. Couldn't let her take up space, rent free.

I deserved better. I deserved my mates. My pack.

There were still times when I still felt unworthy of all this. But if the Goddess had sent them to me, didn't that, by default, make me the only person who was worthy?

When we got home, the guys worked on the new coop for the quail chicks, and I went about the very important task of naming them all.

From a quick glance, they all looked the same— but they were each just different enough that I could pick them out.

"I think this one I should call Wilder," I said, holding up the adorable cuteness.

He turned and looked at me like I was ridiculous.

"See, right here? There's a speck that's the same color as your hair."

He came over and looked. "I approve," and went back to work.

That was all the encouragement I needed. They each got a quail named after them because, well, it made me smile.

And after the stress of seeing Reyna...I needed a smile something fierce.

"I want to ask you guys something," I said. The coop was almost finished, and this question had been brewing in my mind for far too long.

Instantly, they gave me their undivided attention.

This probably wasn't the place to be talking about it... Work still needed to be done, but once the thoughts of Reyna faded, the visions of what I'd noticed wouldn't leave me alone. Better to say something than let it simmer.

"Some of the shifters gave you guys looks," I said. "Is that because you're DarkShadow?"

I tried not to ever say bastard pack, even though that's what most people called them.

"Or was it because of me?" I hated to say it, to even think it, but I couldn't help wondering if I was the reason they were looked at with such disdain.

"Oh, honey, it wasn't you," Vargas said. "We're Darkshadow. We're the bastard pack. We're the ones everyone's scared of—the ruthless ones who'd tear you limb from limb if you crossed us."

Laughter bubbled up from inside me.

"What, you think it's funny?" he asked.

"Since I've been here, you've done nothing but be kind to me. Spoil me. Treat me like I have worth. Not once have I thought of you as ruthless. Not once have I been scared. Sometimes I've been embarrassed—but that's because I'm me."

"That's because you're one of us," Penn said. "You're our family, Rumor."

Just then, Wilder, the quail, hopped out of his box and started running, and the conversation was over as I chased him, herding him toward their new home. Penn's words stayed with me until I went to bed.

In the beginning, I was happy for the bedroom, the nest they made me. It was a sanctuary. It was mine.

Now, it was lonely.

And tonight, I struggled to get to sleep. But worse than that, I struggled to stay asleep.

A night terror ripped through me so horribly I wasn't sure at first if it had been real. A wolf, teeth bared, leaping for me. It was a nightmare I'd had as a child, and for some reason, it had come back today, same wolf and everything.

I tried all the tricks I knew—putting my head on the other side of the bed, turning onto my side, my back, counting to fifty, telling myself dad jokes I'd heard, anything and everything. Nothing helped. I couldn't settle.

So instead, I got up and tiptoed to the bedroom closest to me.

I opened the door.

Penn shot up—wide awake. "Rumor, are you okay?"

"Yeah," I said, still standing in the doorway, but it wasn't true. My head was spinning. I was far from okay. "Can I sleep with you? I had a bad dream."

"Of course." He pulled the covers back, and I padded over, shutting the door softly behind me. I climbed in close, straight into his arms, needing his warmth, needing his scent.

I was getting used to my pack's touch—hugs, a gentle hand on the small of my back, a caress of my check. But this? This was new.

They always talked about my scent...but theirs? Such a draw. Each with a subtle difference, but all three with an undertone of amber...my favorite.

"Do you want to tell me about your nightmare?" He brushed the hair from my forehead, tucking it behind my ear.

"No. I don't want to—" Instead of finishing the sentence, I leaned in, brushing my lips against his.

A short kiss.

Then another.

A third—this time opening my mouth just a little.

And when his tongue ran lightly along my lip, I found myself at a crossroads. Either lean into it and accept everything he was offering, or pull back and

106

take it slow. I wasn't sure there was a middle road. At least not if he kept making me feel this good.

But honestly, I still didn't know how any of this would work.

He wasn't my only mate. And I didn't want to mess things up. So I pulled back.

"I'm sorry," I whispered.

"No, don't be sorry," he said gently. "I like kissing you."

"But what about the others? Will they be mad?" I refused to do anything that would upset them. They were all so special to me, each in his own way.

"No. They might be jealous, though—might wish they were the ones kissing you—but they wouldn't be mad. We know you're ours." There'd been no hesitation to his answer.

"I-I've never done anything like this." It was so embarrassing to talk about, even with him, but he needed to know.

"You mean sleeping in the same bed as a man?"

I shook my head. "I mean, yes, that's new too, but I meant…"

"Having mates?"

I shook my head again.

He lifted my chin to meet his gaze. "What do you mean, Rumor? Because I don't want to keep guessing wrong. And it feels important."

"I've never been kissed before," I admitted quietly. "Never...any of this."

"Is this what you want? Do you want to kiss me?"

"Yeah." More than anything. I was already longing to lean back in and taste his lips.

"Then I want you to touch me. Hold me. But that's all I'm ready for. Is that okay?"

His smile softened. "That is a gift. You gave me your kiss. How could I ever think that was less than okay?"

I sealed my lips to his again, this time a little braver, letting his tongue explore my mouth, letting mine explore his. My hands ran along the muscles of his shoulders and down his back.

I was feeling things I'd never felt before.

Places where I'd never felt anything before were suddenly alive.

And this pulse, this ache, this wetness…this need for more.

I was so glad I'd set boundaries before we started—because now, the lines were blurring, and it would be so easy to sink into something I might regret later. Not because it was him but because I hadn't really thought it all through yet.

And just when I thought things couldn't get any hotter—

His hand slipped down the front of my pajamas.

And, oh my Goddess—

They got a whole lot hotter.

I'd never thought for a moment that fingers could feel this way, stroking gently but firmly, finding just the spot that sent me flying. Growing up, most shifters are aware of sexual things, are not discouraged from exploration. But not in our family. At least, not me. Even though I didn't present as omega until eighteen, I'd never been alone with a male in any sort of intimate situation.

My sister?

Different, I'd learned when I walked in on her once with a boy—not one of her eventual pack.

But I came to these males completely innocent, and as he strummed my most private places, I learned more than in all my years so far.

Chapter Fifteen

Penn

When I woke up, Rumor had already left.

For a moment, I wondered if it had all been a dream—a blissful, wonderful dream. But her scent was still heavy in the air. And all I could think about was the way her soft lips felt against mine.

The way she trusted me in a way she'd never trusted anyone before.

The way she came undone beneath my fingers.

The way she tasted on my lips when I licked them clean—and the way she blushed. That beautiful, adorable blush.

Her curves caught my attention the very first time I saw her. But yesterday...yesterday, I got to explore them. I got to feel her up close. She'd nibbled on my lips, sighed those happy little sounds, welcomed my fingers inside her. She—

I was hard, and she wasn't even in the room. Or maybe I was still hard from last night.

Without consciously deciding to, I reached down into my sleep pants, just to give some pressure, to relieve the ache. But when my fingers wrapped around my length, I imagined it was Rumor's hand. Her scent was still close, saturating my sheets, my skin, my thoughts.

I replayed last night—our first kiss, her whispered moans, the way she fell apart in my arms—as I stroked myself, not even trying to hold back. Her name was on my lips when I came, coating my hand, streaking up my chest.

That's when I noticed her.

Rumor was standing in the doorway, her eyes wide—and then falling to the floor the second she realized what she'd walked in on.

"Good morning, beautiful," I said gently.

She had no reason to be embarrassed. Neither did I. She was my mate. Of course it was her I was thinking about.

"I came to get you for breakfast," she said, flustered. "I thought you were still sleeping."

"I wasn't sleeping," I told her, my voice softer now. "But I was thinking of you."

Her cheeks flushed deep rose. "When you did that…you were thinking of me?"

"Only you."

She stood there for a moment, as if unsure of what to do. Honestly, I wasn't either. What I wanted was to ask her to come in, to stay. Let me wrap myself in her scent a little longer. But I was a sticky mess, and she'd made breakfast.

"I'll be down in a few minutes," I told her.

She nodded and left, still so shy even after last night. Adorable.

When I came down, she was kneading dough— maybe for bread, maybe for pizza—but either way, she was working that dough like it owed her money. My breakfast was already on the counter, waiting for me.

"You made this?"

She shook her head. "No, it was Vargas. But it's good—he's a very good cook." He really was.

"What are you baking?"

"In theory, sourdough," she said. "I tried to make my own starter. Jury's still out."

"It looks great. It looks like dough. I like dough."

She giggled. Gods, what a beautiful sound.

Her phone rang, cutting off her laughter. "Would you hit speaker? I don't want to cover my phone in flour."

I did…without looking.

I shouldn't have.

Because I recognized the voice instantly.

Reyna.

But she wasn't the confident, venom-tongued sister from before. This time, she was crying. I wasn't sure if it was real or not and even though the right thing would've been to leave Rumor so she could have some privacy, I couldn't move. The draw to protect her was too intense. Something felt off about this call. I just hadn't figured out what yet.

If the tears were real, had something happened to one of their parents? As much as Rumor was lucky to be away from them, they were still her family. And losing family—that would hurt.

Rumor asked her what was wrong a few different ways, her sister ignoring her each time until eventually Reyna blurted it out—she couldn't get pregnant.

Or at least she hadn't yet.

"I—I'm so sorry," Rumor said softly. Sincerely.

"You should be." And there was the venom I'd come to expect from her shitty-ass twin.

"Huh?" Rumor was confused, and she should be. It wasn't like she had anything to do with her sister's fertility.

"You know my mates?"

Rumor's face fell. These were the alphaholes who rejected her. Of course she knew who they were.

"They say your name during sex…all of them."

My stomach dropped. Even if that was true, what did sharing it accomplish? Made Rumor feel like shit. Nothing more. It was difficult to believe those two ever shared a womb.

Reyna's mates—the ones who'd rejected Rumor now wanted her. How could they not? She was perfection. But also, how fucking dare they make that known?

Rumor didn't respond. How could she? What was she supposed to say to something like that? It wasn't as if she was controlling their brains or their mouths. That was an issue Reyna needed to take up with her mates.

"I tried to see you at the farmer's market," Reyna went on. "Are you mated? Are you marked?"

So that's why she'd been there. She hadn't stumbled across Rumor by accident. She'd come to spy.

What the fuck?

"You may want to share what your mates say and do in bed, Reyna," Rumor said, her voice sharp now, cutting. Good for her. "I do not feel the same about mine."

I was so proud of her. She'd never have stood up to her sister like this when I first picked her up.

"But…have you gone into heat?"

I'd had enough. I cupped my hands around my mouth and called out, "Hey, Rumor! We need some help with the quail—Little Wilder escaped again! Hurry up!"

Rumor looked at me like I'd just rescued her from drowning. "I-I gotta go," she said quickly, and hung up. Her eyes shimmered with tears.

The phone rang again. She ignored it.

Then a text buzzed through. *Do you want to come home?*

And our mate—our sweet, sexy mate replied with three words. *I am home.*

Chapter Sixteen

Wilder

When Rumor came out to check on the quail, I instantly sensed that something was wrong. Her movements were stiff—similar to when she first came to us, like she didn't know what was okay to do and what wasn't. What happened?

"They're getting big," I said, making small talk and realizing how obvious I was because, while the quail were growing, they were never going to be big.

"Yeah, they are." There was no effect in her tone, just enough words to answer.

I put my hand on her cheek. "Rumor, what's going on?"

"Nothing. I mean, it's not nothing. My sister called, and it was weird. I need to talk to you guys about it. But also, I need to take care of the birds, and it's just...a lot." She pressed her forehead to mine.

"How about I help you with these little guys, and then we'll go find the rest of the pack and talk about it.

Because I'm getting the sense, and correct me if I'm wrong, but it would be better to get this over with."

"Yeah, okay."

And then she did something I dreamed of but never dared hope for—she pressed a sweet kiss against my lips. It was brave. So brave. And it had my entire body alive, and my wolf wanted out.

We fed the quail together, cleaned up their messes, and ended with Rumor's favorite game: Count the quail. It sounded like an easy game. It wasn't. She might be able to tell them all apart, but I sure couldn't—and they never stayed still. But eventually, we were confident they were all here, and none of the little escape artists had gotten out, which wasn't always the case.

Then we joined the others in the garden, where they were building a raised bed. It was a present for Rumor, one she didn't know was hers yet.

"Pack meeting!" I called out, not wanting to add the burden of starting the conversation to our mate. She was already having a rough enough time.

"Inside meeting or outside meeting?" Vargas asked.

And Rumor sat down. "Here is good."

And really, that's the only reason he asked where we were having the meeting. Because we'd always been on-the-fly kind of meeting people. We didn't have the formal runs and all that gobbledygook some of the larger packs thought necessary.

"Do you want me to start?" Penn reached out and put his hand on hers.

"Yes, please."

Penn told us how her sister had called and how she was acting—what I considered predatory. He had called it weird, but regardless, she'd been asking about mate marks and heat, while at the same time talking about how her mates wanted her sister. That didn't add up to goodness. And it sure didn't add up to sisterly love.

"Do you think we need to do anything?" Rumor asked. "Not like go kill them. Because, you know—"

Vargas chuckled. "That's exactly what I want to do—kill them. At least, my wolf does. He figures we can take 'em."

"I'm sure you can," she said. "But let's skip that."

"I propose that we just leave it...until we know we shouldn't." I wasn't sure it was my best idea, but it was the best one I could come up with.

And this was a very informal pack. We ate together every meal—it's not like we wouldn't have time to talk about it again if someone changed their opinion on the matters at hand.

We all agreed it was best to have a wait-and-see approach.

And then, being me, I forgot to think through my next question, just blurted it out there. "Are you still on suppressants?"

We knew she wasn't on the scent blockers, although she'd worn some when we went to the farmer's market. But suppressants—that wasn't something we'd necessarily know anything about unless she shared.

In a lot of ways, it wasn't our business. It was her body. She got to make the decisions about what happened to it—not only as it related to us but also as it related to her heat cycle. If she wanted to avoid them, then she should. But if she decided it was time for us to have pups, then that was her choice as well.

"Yeah. I'm still on them. Are you mad?"

"Oh no, sweetheart. Never mad." Vargas kissed the top of her head. "Never mad. We would never force you to be on them or off them. You are the one who decides."

"Thank you. Thank—and I know you're probably wondering, but I'm going to tell you. But it's really embarrassing."

"You don't have to be embarrassed about anything with us."

"I know about embarrassment." It was time for me to lighten things up, and I did by talking about the time I farted at the dinner table and it smelled so bad we all had to go wait outside for it to dissipate. It hadn't actually been that bad, but the way I told the story had her laughing again.

123

I could already sense her calming down.

"I want you to know," Vargas began, "that we want you to be ours. And that us saying it's up to you on your suppressant usage isn't our way of stating that we don't want you. You are already ours."

I picked up her hand and kissed the back of it. "And when you're ready for more, we'll be there."

She blushed. We already knew she and Penn had slept together last night—in the same bed, anyway. There were no secrets in our house.

"I was thinking of something," she said. Her gaze was focused on the floor, which meant it was something difficult for her to say. That was one of her big tells.

"I-I want to be with you, too. And I'm ready. But I want to mate you before my first heat. I don't want my first time with you guys to be when I'm in a heat-crazed frenzy. I want to remember every part of it. Does that make sense?"

"Yeah," I said, pulling her onto my lap. "It makes 100 percent sense."

Vargas and Penn flanked me, and the three of us wrapped our arms around her, holding her close.

She was ours.

Chapter Seventeen

Rumor

I flushed my suppressants that night.

I'd have to have no heart at all not to.

And it was important partly because while I wanted to begin our life together in earnest, I wanted to experience lovemaking with these three without the insanity of heat or the dullness of suppressants.

Just to be me and my mates getting to know one another in the sweetest, most natural way. But I still had something to deal with. As I remembered the night before when the three of them had held me in their embrace at the same time, I couldn't imagine deciding who to be with first.

Each of them had such an amazing personality and way of showing me their affection. And they were hot. All of them. If I could split into three people, I'd send one to be with each of them, but alas, a mere omega could not do that. Neither could an alpha, for that matter.

I rolled over in bed and pulled my pillow over my head. No rush, right? They'd all been very clear that they would wait until I was ready to go to the next level, and we were building a sweet life even without sex. Maybe we could go on that way? It would save me having to make a decision that could hurt someone's feelings.

They insisted that wouldn't happen. Everything was my choice. Did they understand how hard it was for me to accept that? Even before the day I disappointed them all by being an omega, my family had never let me do whatever I wanted whenever I wanted.

With whomever I wanted.

I'd had a line to toe, a reputation to uphold. My hair had to be just so, my clothing neat and appropriate at all times. In pack events, my sister and I sat side by side at the head table, if there was one. When we ran, we had our positions side by side right behind our parents at the front of the pack. We played with one another because we were too high up to have other friends, even within the pack. In short, our lives were scripted to suit our parents' vision of the next set of alphas.

What a horrible shock I must have been. I shuddered, as memories of that day tried to seep through, wanting to take over the peace of mind I had just begun to gain. The past would have to stay there as I absorbed the freedom of the present.

And the fact that the three sexiest males I'd ever met were willing to wait forever for me to accept them in my bed. Fortunately for us all, I didn't want to wait any longer, circling me right back to the big question.

Who first?

Vargas.

My wolf had never expressed interest in anyone in my life, not family or friends, but she'd been much more animated lately. But this? *What about Vargas?*

Vargas now. She followed her comment with a snarl, and her claws dug into me from the inside. *Mate.*

Why him? Not that he wasn't great, but they all were.

Then I realized something. *You kept me from having to decide.*

Now.

Now…

I scrambled off the bed and raced toward the door. Decision made, I didn't want to wait any longer either. Grasping the knob, I jerked the door open, but before I could take a step into the hallway, I bumped right into a solid wall of muscle.

"Vargas."

Vargas!

"I thought I heard my name." He was sweaty and out of breath. "I was dreaming of you."

"That must have been some dream."

"It was of you." He bent and swept his lips over mine. "Were you calling, querida?"

"Spanish?"

"My first language, and I rarely have opportunity to use it." He stroked my cheek. "What can I get you?"

I lifted my face to his. "You."

"Rumor, what do you mean?"

I rose on tiptoe to whisper next to his ear. "I want you. Now. Here."

"Yes." He scooped me up in his arms and carried me to the bed. "I'm here."

Vargas wore only boxer shorts, which just registered, but I pointed at them. "Off, please."

He stepped out of them and tossed them onto the bedside chair. "Done. But you're overdressed."

I wore a long T-shirt and panties. "Should I take them off?" Silly question.

"No."

"Excuse me?" He was standing there all naked and sexy and telling me not to get undressed? I'd never seen a naked male cock before, but his was intimidating. "You want me to stay dressed?"

"I want to help you with that." And he did, kneeling beside me and easing the shirt over my head. "Lift your hips, and I'll get those panties off." He was kissing every part of me he revealed, whispering sweet words and telling me how beautiful I was and how much he loved me. My heart swelled to breaking, but when he bent and kissed me between my legs, a whole other set of feelings happened.

"Ohhh…is that okay? I don't…can you?"

Lifting his face, I saw his chin was shiny with my juices. "You're so slick, omega, and you taste amazing."

I trembled, gripping his shoulders, trying to keep from melting completely into the bed. "It's so good."

"It's supposed to be." He lowered his face again, lapping and sucking, two fingers working their way into me. "Mmm."

Pleasure so intense everything went black crashed over me, and I was still shivering and whimpering when Vargas rose up and placed his cock at the slicked entrance of me. His first thrust opened me up, a searing pain that faded into more pleasure…and he pushed into me again and again, faster and deeper with each thrust until he grunted and I felt the hot spill of his cum into my body. Wrapping my legs around him, I held him close as he swelled inside me, his knot tying us together.

As we lay, cuddling, the other guys came in and joined us. We cuddled in a wonderful puppy pile, the closeness so much more than I could have ever dreamed of.

Chapter Eighteen

Rumor

Although I hadn't made love with anyone but Vargas yet, we were sleeping in the bed together, all of us in that amazing puppy pile that night. Nobody was pushing me to go further, and I wanted to absorb one step at a time. Even Vargas had not marked me, yet. But sleeping in their arms was something I'd never dreamed could be so wonderful. I felt safe and warm and cared for.

My wolf hadn't expressed an opinion about anyone else yet.

I woke up late, a few days later. Stretching, I enjoyed the luxury of the big bed all to myself while the scents of bacon and coffee tickled my nose. Although I tried to do as much as I could to get them to let me do more work around the house, they were forever insisting that I wasn't here for that. We were a pack together, and we all did our share.

Climbing out of bed, I padded into the shower and got ready for the day. I'd replaced the rags I arrived in with cute and simple clothes, and today, I chose a flowered cotton top and jeans. I planned to spend some time taking care of the quail and do some gardening in the morning. In the afternoon, we were going to a movie.

I hadn't been to one in years, and I was already looking forward to hot buttered popcorn and a tall soda with lots of ice. Didn't even matter what the movie was. The company was the best part.

We were sitting at the breakfast table over second cups of coffee when the doorbell rang, and I hopped up. "I'll get it."

"You sit down." Penn guided me back to my seat. "I'll go see who is bothering us at this hour. Breakfast time is sacred."

"It is?" I'd never heard that.

"It is in our family...now." He disappeared into the hallway, and a moment later came back in. "Rumor, your sister is here. Do you want to see her?"

"No." I didn't even have to think about it. "Tell her to go back to her kingdom and leave me in peace."

"Now, how is that a way to greet your identical twin?" Reyna swept into the kitchen on a cloud of expensive perfume. "I've missed you."

"Really?" Sarcasm dripped from the syllables. "And why is that. Having trouble getting servants?"

She plopped down on Penn's empty chair next to me. "Can we have some privacy?"

"Why would I want to be alone with you?" Except to speed things along maybe.

"Really. I wasn't the one who wanted you sent away. And to here…to them… Well, you know."

"Maybe that's something you should have thought about when you had me waiting on you hand and foot, doing your laundry and making your bed and cleaning your bathroom."

"None of that was my doing, and I couldn't make it stop. Isn't it worth something that I came all this way to make up with you and make sure you weren't being abused by this pack? Why, they are practically criminals."

"Those are my mates you're speaking of," I snarled. "And you are standing in their home insulting them."

She waved a hand at the three alphas. "They bought you. It's not like a love match."

I could have told her different, but this was neither the time or place. And the longer I argued with her, the longer she'd stay. She'd always thrived on conflict. "What do you want, Reyna? No more nonsense. Just tell me, I'll say no, and you can go back to your ordinary life."

"Rumor, I'm your sister." She thrust out her lip in a pout, but I'd seen this move before. "Can you really just tell me to get out?"

"Yes, but I'm afraid if I do that, you're going to come back again. So, let's resolve your issue. I can't imagine what I have that you don't." Unless it was my men, and she was not leaving with them.

She sniffed, but finally let the childish expression fall away, and a piercing stare filled her eyes. "Fine, you never were one for the niceties. I was just wondering if you were marked yet?"

"What?" That was not a polite question.

"Also, do you think your heat is coming soon?"

"Reyna, I don't know why you are asking me these things, and before you attempt to explain, I can't think of anything I care less about."

"I'm an alpha, Sister, and I will do whatever it takes to ensure I have an heir."

I blinked at her. "Not sure what that means, but it doesn't affect me. Goodbye, Reyna. Have a good life."

My sister gave me one last assessing look before turning to stalk out the kitchen door. I heard her voice and Penn's before the front door clicked closed and he returned to the kitchen. "You okay, female?"

"No…yes. I will be, but for right now, I need you to help me forget everything. Can you do that?"

Penn's smile was as bright as the first time we met as he led me upstairs. When he started for my room, I paused. "Can we go to yours?" No real reason, except I wanted him right then and there. No delays. "Now?"

"You sure, omega? You seem pretty upset." He hesitated not because he didn't want me—everything about him told me that wasn't true—but because he was too kind to take advantage of the situation.

"I'm sure." I grabbed his hand and tugged. "Make love to me, but no marking."

"Whatever you say." He strode forward and was soon pulling me up the stairs. "I have been dreaming of you."

He led me into his room and kicked the door closed behind us, sending me tumbling onto his bed. Clothing flew, this time, and I participated fully. I no longer had any fear of the act because I'd been there with Vargas, but I soon learned that the members of this brotherhood were anything but identical in the bedroom. When Penn bent me over the mattress and took me from behind, my slick let him in deep right away, and I found out that an angle could make things very different. It didn't hurt, exactly, but the places he stroked inside me at this angle were very different from Vargas' technique with me, and when Penn reached around to find my pleasure bud, he sent me into a spiraling orgasm, followed by another and another until I felt like I was lost in deep space, everything black or sparkling. His knot swelled so big, I didn't know how there was room for it in there.

After we finished, he carried me into the bathroom and gave me a sponge bath, his tender care getting me so horny, I ended up seducing him again in the shower. And then we had to wash up all over again.

So hot.

But so loving.

Chapter Nineteen

Rumor

I'd been hot and bothered all day, feeling unaccountably uncomfortable in my own skin, and Wilder came in to find me in the kitchen gulping ice water. I'd just changed my panties again, slicking like nobody's business, but I was also feeling guilty.

Wilder…was the last one. Not deliberately. My wolf hadn't even picked Penn for the last one; he'd just come into the kitchen at the right time. And Wilder? No matter how kind he was or understanding, I didn't want him to feel like I cared about him any less than the other two.

"Hi." I set the glass down and prepared to address the issue on my mind. "Wilder, I'm glad you came in. I know we haven't, that is the others…"

He smiled and shook his head. "When you're ready it will be soon enough. But your scent is strong, and I think your heat will be upon you soon."

And I didn't want to wait until that time to make love to him.

"Take your time, but have that in mind, okay?" He pressed a kiss to my cheek and grabbed a can of soda from the refrigerator. "See you later." And he was gone.

He could often be found in the media room at the back of the house reading or playing video games, and often with a snack at hand.

Our nerdy guy was a little big tubby, and a little shy about his body. While the other two often wore only jeans or shorts in the house or gardens, Wilder chose to wear a shirt, but I didn't find him any less appealing for his big of a belly. He had more of a dad bod, but I secretly loved that about him. Substantial. Protective. And he was the best hugger of all.

I followed the sounds of crashing cars and shrieking females into the media room where, sure enough, my mate was playing the newest game. He'd been waiting for this version for over ten years and had just gotten the download last night.

But I'd forgotten about that—somewhat distracted by a whole different kind of gaming the night before in Penn's bed. *Look at me getting all sassy about making love with my pack.* But I remembered as soon as I stepped inside. I couldn't ask him to stop doing something he'd waited so long for, so I turned quietly to leave.

"Omega?" His voice carried over the screeching of tires. "Did you want something?"

"Oh no, just gonna say hi." *Liar.* "Go back to what you were doing before someone…runs you over?"

The sounds cut off, and he pushed his gaming chair back from the desk. "Happens every few minutes. It's less painful than it sounds. Want to try?" He patted his thighs. "Come sit down, and I'll show you how it works."

"Oh, I don't know." I balked. "I've never played, and I'll just mess up your scores or however it works."

"Baby, you really do need a lesson. Come on and try."

It wasn't what I had in mind, but he had no way of knowing that. "It's your funeral." I approached and eased onto his legs. "Complete amateur here."

He gave me a controller and showed me how it worked, and I died in the game over and over until finally he was laughing so hard, I nearly slid off his legs.

"You're enjoying my incompetence way too much," I groused. "I have half a mind to practice and get good enough to beat you."

"Would you?" His voice was soft, and I turned to see his expression soften. "Would you really practice and play with me?"

"I'd like that." I leaned back against him. "But for now, I think I've done enough damage. I'd better go do something useful."

"Like what?" He lifted me and turned me to face him. "I think this is pretty useful. Seriously, you didn't just come in here to say hi, did you?"

My cheeks heated as I remembered what I'd had in mind when I arrived. "Not exactly, no."

"Then? What did you need? Want something built?"

Leaning in to him, I whispered, "Not exactly. I was going to seduce you."

The look he gave me had me blushing harder but also unsure if I should be insulted. "You wanted to…really?"

"Yeah, is that okay?"

"Omega." He kissed my forehead and grasped the hem of my T-shirt. "That's more than okay."

"Wait, shouldn't we go somewhere more private?" I wasn't quite ready to have one of them see me doing things with another, I didn't think.

"Penn and Vargas are cutting up a downed tree at the far side of the property. They're gone at least until lunch, so if you don't object to making love in the flickering light of my game, I don't want to waste another minute."

His kiss was coaxing and sweet, at first, but then deeper, searching, and he only broke it to pull my T-shirt over my head. I hadn't even put on a bra this morning, so as soon as the shirt was gone, my breasts, nipples peaked from exposure to the cool air-conditioning or maybe something else, were in his hands.

"Rumor, you're shaking."

"Am I?"

I leaned back in his hold and his lips descended to take possession of my breasts, sucking and licking, biting just hard enough to draw a mewl from me. Then he lifted me and pushed his screens aside to lay me on the desk and work my pants off. My breathing was harsh, my heart pounding in my chest. The sounds of his game were a cacophonous musical backdrop to everything going on in real life.

Wilder kissed my thighs and my belly then planted one right between my legs before standing up in front of me. If the others had been well endowed, this gaming builder had been gifted by the Goddess.

And no matter how slick I was, I feared I might not be able to accommodate all of him.

"You're so beautiful," he said, pinching a nipple between his finger and thumb. "And so responsive."

I whimpered, having no ability to make words happen right now. His attention to my aching breasts, the broad head of his swollen cock working its way between my folds, and the light flickering all around us absorbed me. I'd never have said a video game was romantic music, especially this kind with all the tire and engine sounds, but it all blended together into an erotic blur, and I forgot about my fear of his fitting because he did.

Gradually, stretching me, my slick making it possible, this man who was a little less confident about his body used it to bring me to powerful orgasms, one after another, as I screamed out his name. My legs wrapped around his hips, and I reached above me to grab the edge of the desk while he drove into me with such power, it stole my breath.

I was close to passing out when he finally reached his apex and filled me with first his cum then this knot, and I came yet again.

Wilder eased me back onto his lap, still connected to me by his knot, and we cuddled together while people in a video game city careened around corners

147

and bounced off walls. Or whatever they were doing. He liked it, and I was going to learn to play too. Anything I could do with one of my mates was great.

We were still there when the other guys came back to make lunch, but by then, we were playing again.

The twists and turns of life with my mates was never going to bore me.

Chapter Twenty

Penn

The morning after Rumor and Wilder were together for the first time, she came padding into the kitchen where we alphas were having breakfast, her cheeks red and a sheen of sweat on her forehead. Her scent preceded her, stronger and more floral than usual.

Her heat was coming on strong. She'd wanted to be with us before this happened, and looked like she'd just made it.

"Good morning, Rumor." I went over and gave her a soft kiss. She leaned into it, lips parting to deepen the kiss. Much more assertive than she'd been before. "What would you like for breakfast?"

"Nothing," she bit out. "Coffee."

Oh, yeah, it was definitely in full force.

"Come sit down," Wilder urged, "and have some toast and jam at least. You need to keep up your strength with your heat."

"Yeah?" She swiped at her forehead with the back of her hand. "I'm just so hot. If this is what it feels like, no wonder suppressants are used. I just took a cool shower, and I think I need another one already. Between the sweat and the slick...I can't imagine feeling less attractive."

Vargas smirked. "You look pretty hot to me, and not hot in a bad way."

"How can you say that? I must just look so gross."

"Anything but," I murmured. "You know how heat works right? It makes the female want her mates but also the mates go wild for her. The scent alone had me stiff as sticks."

"Is that an expression?" Vargas asked. "Remember, English isn't my first language."

"I don't think so. I just made it up."

"Whatever. It isn't helping me to get past this misery." Rumor marched over to the sink and stuck her face under the stream of water. "This sucks so much."

Wilder gave us both a look, and we nodded. "Rumor, before you go in any deeper, we'd like to ask you something."

"Sure, what?" She sounded less tense now. "Anything."

"If you're in agreement, we'd like to mark you and take care of your heat before you get any deeper into the haze."

"After breakfast," I added.

"And that's what I need my strength for?" She started to protest then stopped. "Okay, toast and eggs and bacon because I will need a lot of strength for this, I think."

I was making basted eggs using the bacon grease when Rumor's phone buzzed on the counter.

"Could you get that for me?" she asked. "It's probably just spam."

Sad, but she really didn't have anyone but us to call her. She'd been totally cut off from her whole life except her friend Lily who had managed to call a couple of times.

"I've got it." I was closest. "Oh, what the hell?" I read the text and handed the phone to Rumor. "Just delete it."

151

She frowned, but when she read the screen, she just shook her head. "Why?"

"I don't know, but let's enjoy our breakfast and not think about it too much."

"It's insane," she muttered, but helped herself to a slice of toast just as I slid the plate of eggs and bacon across the table to her. "I don't understand her at all anymore."

After we ate, Rumor wandered off to shower and dress, and I was alone with the other alphas. "What was that?" Wilder asked.

I pushed the phone Rumor left behind across the table to him, and he swiped the screen. "What is this? Why does she want to know if we've marked Rumor? If her heat has come on. They're twins. Maybe Reyna thinks their heats should line up or something? But why would she care? She made it pretty obvious that she has no love for our omega."

"That's a puzzle." Vargas studied the phone in turn and frowned. "But I don't like it. I don't trust that alpha female. It's not like she calls every day to chat up her sister and see how things are going. Her only contacts are like this, demanding personal information in a way that makes me very uncomfortable."

"Agreed." I moved to clear the table, trying to think of a reason that was not sinister. She didn't want to know if they lined up, did she? Did females do that? I'd never heard of such things, but I did have limited experience with females. "I think we need to be extra vigilant with her. That pack was about as sleazy as any I've seen and if they are behind this, nothing good can be happening."

"But she's safe here." Wilder cracked his knuckles. "As long as we're on the homestead."

Chapter Twenty-One

Vargas

We should have stayed on the homestead.

But we needed provisions if we were going to survive three-to-five days of nearly nonstop sex. Wilder hadn't been joking about our omega needing her strength. Actually, we all would, and none of us were going to want to break away and cook elaborate meals. Or anything complicated at all.

We thought about leaving her at home with one of us, but what if there was an attack? Not that we had a reason to expect one, but we were all uneasy enough to prefer to keep her with us all. Also, she wanted to come, and we didn't want to have her worried about anything while she was dealing with the onset of heat.

Rumor had a list of things to pick up while we were in town, and it seemed as soon as we got going, her symptoms eased some. She had begun to like shopping, and we liked to make her happy.

The drive to town, under a bright sun, was cheerful. We were about to enter an intense phase of our relationship, but for now, we were deciding what to buy to eat, what would be easy and fast.

"Sandwiches," Rumor said. "I had to cook so many meals before I came here, and after hours and hours of cooking, I only wanted sandwiches. I couldn't face the things they made me cook."

"Why?" Wilder asked. "Was it something disgusting? Like snails?"

She giggled. "Snails are a delicacy, or so I'm told. But, no. It wasn't that. It was just that after cooking several different meals in one day to please a bunch of ungrateful people who do nothing but complain, I didn't have any interest in eating any of it."

"They complained? After all your hard work?" I was outraged. "You must have wanted to throw it in their faces."

"I wanted to do a lot of things." She looked out the passenger side window of the truck. "But I didn't because what would I do if they threw me out?"

"They never would have," Penn said from the back seat. "You were worth a lot of money to them."

"But I didn't know." She sighed. "If I had, it would have been different. Nobody told me."

"I forgot," he said. "I'm sorry."

"It's okay. I was shocked at first, but when you came for me, I was so relieved. Even though I was thinking that you'd want me to be basically a servant, submissive, and sex toy."

I hated so much that she thought that. What must it be like to feel so entirely out of control of your own life? Your future? "If we ever make you feel like any of those things, you call us out on it. We do not live that way."

"I know." She patted my hand on the steering wheel. "It didn't take long to figure that out. I'm so happy here with the three of you, and soon I'll be marked and we'll really be mated."

"We're mated now," Wilder asserted. "But I can't lie and say I'm not looking forward to marking this pretty neck."

157

She gave a little shiver. "I'm a little uneasy about the heat. It sounds like it spirals out of control."

"Not with us." I stroked her hair and returned my attention to the road. "We won't let that happen to you. Our fathers taught us long ago that omegas are not less than alphas, just different. After all, how would we have children without you."

Penn poked me. "You make her sound like a brood mare."

"That's not what I meant—"

Rumor pushed his hand away from me. "No, I understand, and I appreciate it. You treat me like a person, which means more than you might think."

As we arrived in town, I circled a couple of blocks before finding a good parking space. We all trooped over the grocery store. Rumor had put the list of things we decided on in her phone, and, as we pushed the cart up and down the aisles, she directed us to the various items we needed.

"Frozen lasagna," she said. "And enchiladas. Ice cream." The freezer section was key to our plan, as were sandwich makings and ramen cups. Premade salad. A rotisserie chicken. Usually our food was scratch made, but under these circumstances, we'd be too distracted to do much cooking.

We piled the cart high, checking out and heading for the truck with armloads of bags. "I think we have enough," Penn said. "After we load all this in the truck, I want to make a quick stop at the bakery."

"And I need something from the hardware store," Wilder added. "Vargas, come with me?"

"Deal."

"Would it be all right if I picked up some things from the bath store?" Rumor asked. "I feel the urge for girly supplies."

We looked at one another. That wasn't the plan. We were supposed to be sticking together to keep our omega safe.

"I don't know," I said.

"Why not?" Penn asked. "Rumor, we'll walk you right to the bath store, and you don't come out until one or more of us returns for you. Does that work for you?"

"Yes!" Her cheeks reddened. "If we're going to be handling my heat, I want to at least start out looking and smelling my prettiest."

We finished loading our groceries and other supplies, and the three of us walked her to the bath store and watched her go in before splitting up to run our other errands.

Chapter Twenty-Two

Rumor

It all happened so fast.

One minute, I was looking at bath bombs. The next, I was being thrown into the back of a truck. I didn't even have time to scream, to call for my mates—anything, before we were on the road. They didn't even try to hide who they were, which was terrifying. They had no intention of letting me go.

Once, we were my mates. The ones who rejected me. The ones who thought I was garbage. The ones who chose my sister over me and who were part of the plan to sell me.

And now—now, here they were, taking me, binding my hands, binding my wrists, and scenting me repeatedly.

"What the fuck!" I tried to squirm out of their hold.

I wouldn't have had the strength to stand up to them like that before. I wouldn't have had the strength to do anything but cower beneath them. I was just an omega after all. A piece of trash to be discarded, one with no power.

And maybe that's what they were counting on, my weakness.

There were growls, but nothing more. Intimidation tactics weren't going to work on me. I finally had something to fight for, and I planned to do exactly that—fight.

"What the fuck are you doing?"

All of my rejected mates were in the back with me. But they weren't alone. No. When I saw who was driving, it was so much worse than that.

Reyna was behind the wheel. Fucking Reyna. My twin.

"Reyna, tell them to let me go." I was her sister. She might not like me or my designation, but that didn't change the fact that we shared a womb before we ever took our first breaths.

"Shut up, omega, before we make you." Reyna didn't even say my name, and that was enough to tell me loud and clear that she wasn't going to help me out of this. If anything, she was the one behind it.

And worst of all, I could hear there was truth in her words. She would make me.

They would make me.

I needed to pull back, to fall in line with the behavior I adopted as an omega, become the person I used to be. At least until I could figure out how to get out of this mess. But first, I needed to figure out why I was here in the first place. Had she found a second buyer for me? Was she trying to double her profit? Was it more sinister than even that?

"They don't want me. They already rejected me. You rejected me. Let me go. I won't get in your way ever." I really sucked at shutting up.

"None of us want you. No one wants you. Now shut up. You have been warned."

This time, I did stop talking in the hopes my true mates would already be on their way to help me. The odds were slim. My sister had choreographed my kidnapping like a boss. But they loved me, and I was pack. They would find a way.

But even if they didn't, if her plan was far too good, I needed to be smart about things. I had to be prepared in case there was a window where I could fight and possibly escape. Why didn't I ask my mates to teach me how to fight? That would come in so handy about now.

When we reached our destination, I wasn't surprised we were on my old pack lands. What did surprise me was, they brought me to the freaking barn, of all places.

Did my parents know this was happening? Was that why I was here instead of at their house? Because, deep down, Reyna knew this was wrong—and they would stop her?

But, would they? There was no love lost there. They didn't want me or need me. Or even like me. I was a point of shame in their lives, nothing more.

No. Being out here was for some other reason.

They threw me on a pile of hay, and not for my comfort. It likely just happened to be there. Because the next thing I knew, they were chaining me to the wall. If they wanted me comfortable, that was not how to do it.

I wanted to scream, to cry for help, but there'd be no one to hear me. And if I did, they would shut me up, which I had a feeling meant either gagging me or harming me.

Neither was good.

I needed to be quiet. Compliant. I needed to be the omega they wanted me to be, at least for now.

My sister came over to me, checked my bindings, and then cackled.

She fucking cackled.

"Well. At least you're good for something." And she walked away.

Everyone left me there in the barn. But I could hear someone outside. I wasn't sure who it was, but they were there.

Maybe Lily would have a chore that needed doing out here. Maybe she would help me.

I'd help her too.

We'd get out of here together. And my mates would take her in. They'd help her be safe, maybe help her find her own mate.

That was my best bet right now. My sister forgetting Lily had business down here and the timing being perfect. It might be my best bet, but it wouldn't be a good one.

But the more I thought about it, the more I saw how unlikely it was for my mates to look here. My pack didn't want me. They made that clear. Them stealing me back was the last scenario they'd consider.

I didn't know how many hours passed before Reyna came back.

She held a cup in her hands, one with both a lid and a straw. It was pink, thick-ish, and almost medicinal looking. Like maybe a milkshake that had gone bad.

"Drink." It was a command.

"Is this wolfsbane?" I needed to know if it was time to fight because it was better to go out fighting than go out drinking poison.

"No. It's vitamins. Protein. Nutrition. Hydration drink."

I wasn't sure I believed her. But I drank. One sip. Then another. Then another. It was chalky and gross, but the few times I slowed down, she kicked me—first my ankles then my knees. Places that wouldn't knock me out but sure as hell hurt.

"Your heat's coming soon."

I knew that. But why did she sound like that was exciting information?

"And when it gets here," she seethed, "you're going to finally have a purpose."

She couldn't possibly mean what I thought she did. "I have mates, Reyna."

"No, you don't. If you did, they'd have marked you. They think of you as the piece of trash you are. Try again."

She was right on one point. They hadn't marked me. But that was mostly on me. They were so careful, making sure every step was my choice. And now, that was coming back to bite me in the ass.

167

"They'll come find me." I wasn't sure I believed that, but if the plan wasn't to kill me but to take advantage of my heat somehow, it was worth the risk.

"They have no idea you're here, omega. Besides, you owe it to your pack."

"This isn't my pack, they are. What could I possibly owe you? You've been paid."

"Your womb."

"What the fuck are you talking about?" Deep down, I knew, but admitting it to myself was too much.

"I need heirs. And you are going to provide them for me."

And suddenly that phone call started to make sense. She couldn't have children, and she was betting on me being womb-erific. Fuck her.

"No, I won't."

"You have no choice. If I don't have heirs, I lose this pack. And you." She pointed at me "You share my DNA. You're my twin. My mates can fill you with a baby, and then, you know what? It's mine. No one will know, not even with human testing."

She was disgusting.

"And I will have control of this pack."

"You're fucking evil."

"I'm your sister." Which didn't make my evil diagnosis any less true.

"No. I'm your alpha. And you will do as I say." She kicked my knee one more time and walked out of the barn, leaving me alone to contemplate my fate.

Chapter Twenty-Three

Wilder

I was the first one back at the bath store and, when I went inside, I didn't immediately see her. After calling her name and getting no response, I followed her scent, only to have it lead straight to an emergency exit.

My heart raced. My wolf freaked out. I pushed the door open, and an alarm blared.

"I told you to keep that door shut!" the woman behind the counter yelled.

"Who?" I asked. "Who needed to keep this door shut?"

She looked from her task. "Oh. Sorry. I thought you were those other guys."

"Other guys?" My wolf was so close to the surface I feared the employee would see him.

"Yeah. They came and got their friend." She went back to labeling the bath bombs she'd been working on.

"Their friend… Was their friend a beautiful woman?" *Please let it be another guy and Rumor was just in the bathroom.*

"Yes, with long hair and a red shirt."

Fuck. Fuck. Fuck.

Before I could ask for more information, Vargas came in. "Where's Rumor?"

"I think we have a problem." I told him what the woman had said, and the two of us ran straight out the back door, not even caring that the employee would be pissed. Let her be.

We followed our mate's scent through the door, out to the alley and then, just like that, the scent ended. The only thing left of her, her phone.

She was gone.

"We need to find Penn," Vargas said. "And we need to get our mate back."

Vargas told me to get Penn from the bakery across the street. He'd go back in and talk to the woman.

My heart was pounding so hard, it echoed in my ears. My thoughts spiraled to the worst places. I grabbed Penn and came back, and by then, Vargas had a few details: number of people and what they were wearing. But her description of their faces? Pretty much useless—they were handsome, whatever the fuck that meant.

Vargas had asked about cameras, something I'd not even considered. But, of course, they didn't have any. That would've made our next step too easy.

We were fucked.

"We need help. We have no clues, no trail to follow, and no tracker to trace." Vargas sounded as defeated as I felt. "Not the police."

We were all in agreement on that. Without any proof she actually was taken, they wouldn't care anyway. Not until more time had passed, and I wasn't willing to wait.

"What about the Black Wings?" Penn asked. "They control a lot of this area. And they're all, like, fancy-pants with their tech."

He was right. They were our best bet. We didn't want to lose a second's time and went straight to their pack lands, not even bothering to ask permission to be on their land. This was an emergency…an ask-

173

forgiveness situation. We didn't have time for formalities.

They technically did owe us a few favors. Wilder had helped them with a livestock issue, and Vargas had helped rebuild one of their buildings after a tornado. We didn't usually get along with other packs or interact with them at all, for that matter. We kept to ourselves, wanting to avoid the looks and treatment we got from others. But, if we had friends? These were them.

We pulled up to the gate and one of the wolves was standing there on all fours. I stepped out of the truck.

"We need help," I said. "Our mate…our mate was kidnapped."

He growled, and I thought we were screwed, but then he shifted to his skin, and we told him what happened.

"I'll meet you at the main house. We can discuss this situation there."

He arrived before we did and brought us into their dining room where a handful of wolves joined us, all

174

listening to us tell them what happened and asking questions. Some felt irrelevant, but maybe they knew something we didn't and they mattered.

There was a lot of back-and-forth on how to figure out who took her, especially without store cameras. Those cameras, or lack thereof kept coming up, and the alpha who greeted us at the gate, Ray, called for the pack's tech guy—his name was Max.

Max looked more like a linebacker than a tech nerd, but he grabbed the computer and started typing. From what I could see, the screen was filled with more numbers than words. I had no idea what he was doing, but then again, I wasn't a tech specialist. He was.

My packmates and I stood there. We didn't ask questions. None of us wanting to break his concentration, which appeared intense.

Max slammed both palms onto the table. At first, I thought it was in frustration, but then his smile grew. "I'm in."

"Not your fastest," the pack alpha teased. Is that what we were doing? Having a good time?

Vargas didn't think so. His wolf was growling in his chest.

I placed a hand on his shoulder to calm him. This wasn't the time to get angry and reckless. If there was ever a time Rumor needed us to use our brains, it was now.

"So…this is actually the bakery across the street," Max said. He blew part of it up so we could see the reflection of the baked goods in the glass. "But if we look across…is that the alley?"

I nodded.

"Okay. Exactly how long ago was this?"

We gave our best estimate. He rewound the footage.

A van pulled up. Men got out—their faces obscured. Even the one who walked around to the front to open the door for the others had his head down and a hood up. They were prepared. This wasn't spontaneous.

Less than a minute later, the alarmed door opened. Two men went inside, and the three of them came out a minute later carrying our mate. She was struggling. Fighting. Good girl.

Then the driver's side opened, and the woman who had been behind the wheel walked around to open the back doors.

Unlike the others, she didn't hide her face.

It was Reyna.

Reyna had taken our fucking mate.

Reyna had stolen her own twin.

Reyna needed to die.

"What does she want with her?" Penn asked.

"Remember when she texted? How she asked questions about Rumor's heat?" I hated to even think the two were connected, but it was the only thing that made sense.

This time, the growl in Vargas's chest turned into a deep, rumbling sound. I could smell his fur—he was right at the edge.

So was I.

"We need to get her," I barked. "We need to bring her back, and we need to do it fast. Her heat's almost here, and I don't know what they're going to do to her." My voice cracked. My eyes blurred. "But we can't let it happen."

We hadn't even told her we loved her yet. Not in those words. And already we'd let her down.

We'd failed her.

But we wouldn't do it again.

I refused.

We were going to get her back. We were going to make her officially our omega. We were going to mark her and let the entire world know that she was fucking ours. And that anyone who even looked at her wrong would pay the ultimate price.

Chapter Twenty-Four

Rumor

I'd been moving into heat when they took me, but somehow it was slowing down now that I was here. All the warmth and aching, the sweat and irritability that I'd been suffering was abating. Maybe because it was the least of my problems. Or because I was away from my alphas.

My sister and her pack kept coming in and checking on me, waiting for me to go into heat, and I just shrugged their inquiries off. Heat? What heat?

As far as they were concerned, I had no symptoms whatsoever. Never had and never would. If I could hold out long enough, maybe they'd believe I was as infertile as Reyna. But then what would they do?

I found that out soon enough.

"I would have sworn she was close to going into heat," I heard Reyna say to one of her pack. "But I see no signs of it now."

That's right. No signs at all.

"Then you might as well let me go," I said. "Because I'm no use to you."

"It's not that easy, Sister," Reyna said. "Eavesdropping? I thought you were asleep."

"How can I sleep with you gossiping right outside the door." I sat up straight, bound hand and foot, wrists and ankles ragged from trying to escape. "I guess we're both infertile, and you'll have to get your heir somewhere else."

"We still have steps to take." She tapped her foot on the dirt floor. "I was even going to let you mate with my mates, which should be a real treat after the dregs you've been with. But we can't do that yet."

I pushed my anger down. It felt far too much like heat, and I didn't dare display any symptoms or things they could pretend were symptoms. "I'd rather die than let one of your sloppy seconds manhandle me. No point, anyway, since I'm not in heat."

"You will be, as soon as the heat accelerator Mother ordered arrives. She says it's how she got pregnant with us. Seems we have some kind of a genetic flaw. Who'd have guessed it?"

Considering how I was treated when I presented as an omega, I certainly never would have expected any kind of tolerance at a genetic or any other kind of flaw in our family. Mother dear would have a lot to answer for if I ever planned to speak to her again. Which, of course, I would not.

But a heat accelerator? One more thing about the birds and bees I knew nothing about. This one chilled me to my bones. If it worked, I'd be pregnant by one of my sister's pack and probably kept around for multiple pregnancies, a fate far worse than death. How could she do this? Was her drive to succeed stronger than any kind of feelings toward me? Not that I expected kindness, but subjecting me to a lifetime of rape and bearing children who would be ripped from my arms and placed in her cold, unfeeling ones? That was far beyond what I'd expected from her. "And if I'm a good girl, maybe you'll let me nanny to 'your' children?"

Her eyes grew wide. "I never thought of that. What a good idea. Of course, you could never tell them the truth, and once they were old enough to understand you'd, never be allowed to see them again. But it's certainly handier than having to buy formula or hire a wet nurse."

My Goddess, she was taking me seriously. She'd lost the last bit of her soul in her ambition. "So, Mother knows you can't have children? She knows I'm out here tied up to be sacrificed for your career goals?"

She waved a hand in dismissal. "No she doesn't. I told her the accelerator was for me because I was ready to be a mom and my heat was slow in coming. What kind of a mother do you think she is?"

"A lot like you would be, if you were to have any children."

She actually preened. Took it as a compliment. I struggled harder, the ropes carving deep wounds into my flesh. If couldn't get out of here, I would have to find another way to escape her plans. My wolf howled inside me, but I shushed her, promising I had no idea of ending my life. Why should Reyna get to live on if I didn't? The only way I was dying in this scenario was if they killed me.

Did my mates know where I was? Surely, after all the questions from my sister about heat and such, they wouldn't have a hard time figuring it out. And Reyna's pack would be expecting them to try, wouldn't they?

Fat tears coursed down my cheeks at the thought of anything happening to them.

"And don't be expecting those bastards of yours to come and rescue you. We're ready for them, if they do. Not that you're worth their trouble, but just in case." I'd have said she read my mind, but we'd never been that kind of twins.

Rage supplanted fear and grief. "If you harm my mates, I will never rest until you're dead in pieces at my feet." An image my wolf enjoyed way too much.

Was that the solution? Shifting? Why hadn't I thought of it before? The act should be sufficient to free me from the ropes. Maybe. I closed my eyes and summoned my wolf, but while I could feel her there, she was not coming forth. I struggled harder, as did she, before she lapsed back down deep. Why?

"What else was in that drink? You lied to me. It wasn't just supplements or whatever you said. That odd taste?"

183

"Oh, shifting suppressant, just a dash. I was afraid too much would keep you out of heat. Mother has quite the medicine chest. How do you think they control the larger pack?"

Fuck.

"Were you born evil, or did something happen when I presented as omega to make you hate me this much?" I leaned my back against the wall, studying her face, so much like mine and yet different in ways that only emotions could carve. Even this young, her expressions were set in dissatisfaction and meanness.

"Hmm, I could ask you if you were always this helpless and pathetic, but I won't. We both know the answer. We were supposed to rule together, but that's obviously off the table. You're only useful to me as a brood mare and servant now. I have to go up to the house for dinner, now, or Mother will know something is wrong. I think she'd be fine with my plan, but I don't want to bother her with it. And I am not sure what Father would say. Be a good girl and don't make a fuss, and I'll send you down something to eat later on."

Chapter Twenty-Five

Vargas

"You sure nobody saw us cross onto the lands? We'd have known if someone entered ours." Penn crouched beside me in some brush just inside the tree line. We had a good view of the buildings on the land from here.

"No, I can't be sure of anything," I murmured in as low a tone as I could manage. "But I don't see any signs of it."

"Wilder should be back by now." He'd gone in wolf form to reconnoiter about fifteen minutes before. "The alpha house is all lit up, and it must be close to dinnertime. Somehow, I doubt they've invited our omega to eat with them, so they've got to have her stashed around here somewhere."

We'd been afraid three strange wolves tripled our chances of being caught, and Wilder drew the long straw, but if he didn't return soon, I was taking my fur.

A crunch in the dry grass off to my left had me on full alert until I spotted the wolf who'd stepped on the stick. Even in his fur, Wilder was less graceful than we were, but he'd won the right to go search fair and square.

Waiting until he was back in his skin, I asked, "What did you find out?"

"She must be in the barn. I just saw her bitch of a sister and her pack leave there. They put a big padlock on the door and headed up the hill to the alpha house, talking about what they were having for dinner."

"What assholes," Penn growled.

"Goes without saying," I snarled. "But that means this is our one shot at getting her."

"Oh, and listen to this. They are planning to put her on a heat accelerator, and her shift is suppressed as well."

"Better living through chemistry." Penn was on his feet. " Or dying in their case, once we get to them. Let's go."

"We need a plan." I pointed to Wilder. "Get dressed, and we'll let Penn take his fur for the next phase. Here's what I think we should do."

Five minutes later, we'd skirted the barn, keeping to the shadows and the brush as much as possible. The door was indeed padlocked, and we didn't have a crowbar with us, so we did some more searching of the area to find a useful tool. Farms, at least messy ones like this, always had old tools lying around, and I feared the iron bar we came upon was too rusty to do the job, but when I slid it behind the latch, and Wilder and I each took hold of an end, the hinge popped right off. They really needed to take better care of the barn ,or it would end up falling down around their heads one day.

I didn't hate the idea as long as our omega was far away when it happened.

Easing the door open, I cringed at each creak, knowing how sound carried in the quiet of the countryside. A soft gasp had me pivoting and leaping on a figure huddled in a nearby shadow.

"Shhh," I warned. "Another sound, and I'll snap your neck."

"Don't!" Our mate's voice carried to us from the darkness of the structure. "Lily? It's you?"

We knew of her friend and how much Rumor worried about her. I placed my mouth near her ear and hissed, "Shhh. If you're Lily, nod. And if you are lying, well, you know what will happen." Her form was slight, and she was shaking so hard, my wolf registered no enemy.

She nodded, and I moved my hand. "I was bringing Rumor some food, but then I saw the door was locked and I heard you all moving and…" She whimpered. "You're hurting me.

I was holding her too tight, her slight form in danger of severe bruising. "Sorry." I released her.

"Reyna wanted to use Rumor to have babies for her pack."

So that was it? They'd used her as a servant before and now they intended to…to… "Look, you hide back where you were before until we get Rumor out and it's safe, okay?

She nodded again, rubbing her arms, still trembling. "Yes." Melting into the shadows, she made me wonder how often she did that for her own safety or to avoid unwelcome notice.

Penn took up the watch, his wolf's ears twitching with alertness while Wilder and I slipped inside the barn, following the sound of our mate's breathing. When we saw her condition, my wolf's fury was almost beyond controlling. Only the reminder that our mate's safety could be compromised if we went on a rampage and tried to kill everyone on these lands kept him in check.

"Rumor, querida," I soothed, slitting the ropes that dug into her skin with the one tool I always had with me, a pocket knife. "We're taking you home now."

"I don't think so." Reyna laughed, and I turned to see her standing in the doorway with her pack around her. "Leave now, and we'll let you live. We promise not to beat your little bitch too severely, as long as she follows the rules and doesn't cause any trouble."

My wolf burst through the barrier and took control, shredding my clothes as he leapt into battle, followed by Wilder in his fur and Penn. The female stepped back, but her mates also took their fur, and a fierce battle ensured. We were more evenly matched than I liked, but I could see my packmates to either side of me, and I had my fangs poised above one of the male's jugular when he went limp and begged me not to kill him.

The others were no longer fighting either, the cowards, and we could end it, but our mate lay in a heap, unconscious. I saw what I hadn't before, the amount of blood she'd lost from the wounds on her limbs. She'd no doubt been trying to get free, and her scent was all distress.

Suddenly, the weaklings we had bested mattered not at all, and I tossed my opponent to the side and shifted, racing to our mate. "Rumor, querida, hang on and we'll get you out of here."

Her eyes opened halfway as I lifted her into my arms. "Bring Lily. She isn't safe here."

"Yes, of course." I carried her toward the door and out into the night. The alpha house still glowed above us, no sign that anyone had noticed the kerfuffle below.

Did Reyna tell her family what she was up to, or did she somehow think she could kidnap her sister and use her with nobody finding out?

Maybe claim she came back on her own and threaten her with the safety of the children she wanted her to bear or something equally horrible? I wanted to kill them these people slowly and painfully.

"Vargas?" Rumor's faint voice pulled me back to the moment. "They're not worth it."

No they weren't. "Let's go home."

Luckily, we kept some extra clothes in the truck because otherwise we'd have been driving along the highway naked. No shifter let that happen more than once.

Chapter Twenty-Six

Rumor

"Do you need anything, Rumor?" Lily was still hovering as if she were a servant, even though she'd never been that to me.

"No, do you?" I fluffed up a final pillow on my big round bed in anticipation of a very special night with my mates. We'd have done this the moment I got back, but I was so bruised and exhausted, they insisted we wait.

After a couple of nights of rest, we'd all shifted and run the night before, since the shifting suppressant finally wore off. Who knew my mother was not just a manipulator but some kind of chemical expert in controlling females and their heats?

My wolf was blissed out as we raced along the trails on the pack lands and beyond, splashing in streams and rolling around together. When we returned home and shifted back, the deep cuts from trying to get out of the coarse rope bondage had healed, bruises faded, and the first signs of heat were surging back.

Uncomfortable as they were, I welcomed them, wanting more than anything in the world to be fully their mate, marked and, hopefully, carrying their young.

Lily winced at my offer to do something for her. "I can't get used to not being someone's servant. I feel so at loose ends."

"You don't have to be that. You're living here as my friend and one of the family, so I'll tell you what my alphas told me. Help out any way you like, but know it's not expected. And if you want to bake cookies, you will get no complaints from anyone here."

"Cookies? I can do that." She was out the door and headed down the hall so fast, I had to laugh. Everyone liked to be useful, and Lily loved to bake. It was a matter of finding her place in this new part of her life. I welcomed her company but suspected it wouldn't be long before she had a pack of her own. Sweet, kind, and pretty, nothing could hold her back if that was what she wanted.

"Querida?" Vargas stood in the doorway. "May we come in?"

Sitting back on the bed, I smiled up at my three alphas. "Yes, and close the door so we don't shock Lily. She's baking us cookies."

"Nice." Wilder followed Vargas in. "What kind?"

"I don't know." I giggled. "Does it matter?"

"Nope. I like them all." Wilder sat down next to me and lifted my hand to his lips. "But not as much as I love you."

My heart hammered in my chest. "I love you too. All of you. When you bought me from my former family, I was relieved to be away from them, but I never dreamed I'd fall in love. Omegas aren't supposed to get this lucky."

"I don't know why not." Penn sat on my other side and untied the ribbon holding my pale-blue satin robe closed. I'd bought it at the bath store with just this sort of occasion in mind. "I think we're the ones who are lucky. I love you too."

As Vargas pushed my robe over my shoulders, they eased me back to lie on the bed and then stood to take off the lounge pants they all wore. Even Wilder wore no shirt now, since I'd convinced him his body was as sexy as anything I'd ever seen, and when they joined me on the bed, I struggled to get enough air to breathe and stay conscious. Until now, I'd been with only one of them at a time, but for this mating we had agreed we would all be together.

Their hands and lips roamed my body, and I closed my eyes, very aware of who was touching me where when Vargas moved to lie between my legs. Wilder and Penn turned their attention to my breasts, sucking, licking, and nipping while Vargas inserted two fingers inside me, his thumb rubbing my clit in slow, sensual circles. If this was just the foreplay, I'd never survive mating with all three of them. Or maybe, from the hunger I felt, I'd devour them. In the best way possible.

Then his fingers were gone, replaced with his cock, and he was inside me. I writhed, digging my fingers into his shoulders, held in place by the other two or I might have fallen off the bed. Vargas thrust deep inside me, whispering words of love, faster and faster, my slick coating him until he grasped my hips, lifted my lower body off the bed and poured his cum into my body. His knot grew, and I came with him before he lowered me to the bed and bent to sink his teeth into the side of my throat, making me orgasm again.

He held me close, they all did until his knot finally shrank and I demanded Wilder take his place, his own rhythm already familiar and comforting and intense at the same time. Each of them touched different places in my body, my heart and soul, and after Wilder moved aside, his mark on the other side of my throat, Penn turned me over and took me from behind, finding new places to stimulate inside me before he came and pierced the back of my neck to make his mark. I'd come so many times, I was soaked with sweat and unable to so much as move when Penn finally withdrew from me.

They covered me up and left then came and carried me into the bathroom where they'd drawn a bubble bath. An herbal scent tickled my nose. "What is that?"

"Healing herbs. You've been through a lot over the past ten hours." Vargas kissed the top of my head. "We don't want you to be uncomfortable."

"Or raw," Penn put in helpfully.

Sinking into the water, I rested my head on the bath pillow they'd considerately placed there before blinking at them. "Ten hours? Surely not." I only remembered making love with each of them once. After that it was all a haze of pleasure and a little pain and begging them to do it again and again. Oh Goddess.

"It was. How are you feeling?" Wilder asked.

"Good." I flexed my arms and legs. "Fine. A little tired like after a good workout. Are you guys okay?"

"Fine. And the heat?" he asked.

When we began, I'd been sweating and aching. As soon as I got back with my alphas, the heat had come roaring back. But now?

I did an internal search of my body and mind. "I think it's gone. Oh that's not good. What's wrong?" Maybe I was like my sister, infertile. Had she even had

198

heat symptoms? Had she tried that stimulator or whatever she was going to give me?

"Mate, shhh," Penn said. "It's very good. The best."

I yawned, too tired to even think about what it might mean. If they said it was all good, I was ready to accept that as fact. My mates washed me carefully with soft cloths and sweet-smelling soap before drying me tenderly, carrying me off to bed, and crawling in after me. Right before I fell asleep, I heard Wilder say, "Cookies!"

Lily must have come in while we were in the bathroom and left some there. My mates would need their strength. My heat might be over, but my hunger from them was anything but.

Chapter Twenty-Seven

Vargas

I was hitting up the herb garden, grabbing some basil for dinner tonight, when I noticed a new rock in the bed. This one was painted like a little house—but the roof was made of flower petals. I didn't know if it was a gnome home or a tiny fairy house, but Rumor did a beautiful job.

I loved finding her rocks in random places. I thought of them as little messages to let us know she was thinking of us. It was so good to have her back. Just thinking about when she was gone—even for that short period—made me shudder.

And now that she was here, marked, ours, I wanted to keep her in a bubble.

It wasn't fair to her, of course. She wouldn't want that. She told us as much. But that didn't stop my wolf from thinking it was the safest option.

We'd built a little cabin behind the main house for Lily. She was always welcome in our home, too, but she never really had a place of her own before, and we wanted to give her that. We thought it had been hard getting Rumor to realize she didn't have to do everything around here—but with Lily, it was triple the challenge.

She was getting there, though. And it was nice to see Rumor have a friend—someone to laugh with, to do each other's hair, probably to talk about us... Whatever it was girls liked to do.

They were both happy. And, consequently, so were my mates and I.

Back in the kitchen, I started assembling the caprese salad—our mate's favorite. The tomatoes were especially good this year. I sliced and layered them with the basil from the garden. It was the perfect combination.

We were throwing a birthday party for Rumor.

Only she didn't know it yet.

Calling it a party might've been a stretch—it was just us. But I'd baked a cake and made all her favorite foods. We had presents. Not as many as I wanted to give but three very important ones. The ones we had for her before she even came to us. The ones that told her we'd been waiting. That she was ours.

She and Lily came in first, wearing matching sundresses Lily had made out of a bolt of fabric she'd picked up at the farmer's market. They looked radiant.

Rumor crossed the room and pulled me in for a searing kiss. I didn't think it was possible to ever get enough of our omega. When our lips came apart, I noticed Lily looking away, trying to give us some privacy. She was shy like that.

Wilder arrived next, holding a huge bouquet of flowers. He cut them and placed them in a vase on the table while Rumor and Lily set the table.

I wanted to tell Rumor not to help—but she didn't know this was her surprise dinner yet, and even if she did, Rumor tended to get pushy if we told her not to do anything. Even now.

Penn was the last to arrive.

"Sorry I'm late," he said, kissing Rumor on the cheek. "I lost track of time trying to fix the truck. It was making a weird rumbling sound."

203

At least he was freshly showered. Rumor did not love the smell of grease. I didn't either, but Penn didn't care about my preferences. He used to come to dinner covered in grease. But then again, a lot of things were different pre-Rumor.

We all sat down and ate the meal I'd prepared, talking about our day, sharing laughs. Then it was time for cake.

The look on our mate's face when I brought it out, candles lit, and we all sang "Happy Birthday," it filled my heart to the brim.

When it was time to blow out the candles, she looked at each of us and said, "I don't have anything left to wish for. They all came true when you came for me." She smiled. "Lily, I want you to have this one."

Lily didn't need to be asked twice. She took a deep breath and blew out all the candles, and we all cheered.

The cake was strawberry layered with fresh whipped cream. We ate most of it and would probably regret it later with stomachaches, but it was that good. *Yay, good strawberry harvest.*

Then it was time for cleaning up and presents.

Presents we were doing upstairs, just the four of us. We had things to say, things meant only for our mate. As much as we loved having Lily around, sometimes privacy mattered.

After the dishes were cleaned and Lily had left for the evening, we asked our omega to go to her nest and wait for us. We came bearing gifts only a few minutes later.

"I thought you were the gifts," she said, crooking her finger at us.

"We are." I grinned. "But there's also a free gift with purchase."

Wilder laughed. "The day we met you, we knew you were ours. Our only regret is that we didn't mark you sooner. That we didn't tell you how we felt."

"You don't need to apologize for that," she said softly. "You gave me the space I needed. And everything turned out exactly how it should. If Reyna hadn't taken me, Lily wouldn't be here."

She was so gracious and kind, even with all she'd been through.

"This is my gift." Penn handed her his gift bag. "When I first heard there was an omega who needed rescuing—who needed to come home—I made this for you. I didn't know then what I know now. That you were our mate. But I hoped."

She pulled out the tissue paper and found a beeswax candle inside, the kind created by wrapping thin, thin wax sheets that looked like a honeycomb. He had shaped it like a hive.

"It's beautiful," she said and pulled him in for a long kiss. "Thank you."

"Here's mine," Wilder said, handing her a larger gift box.

Inside was a pillow. At first glance, just a pillow—nothing special. Only this one was special. It had been made with down from the geese we used to raise. At the time, we thought they were a good idea. Turned out, they were mean as hell. No love lost when they became dinner.

He told her the story, and she hugged the pillow close. "I'm not sharing this with any of you," she warned. "So don't even try it."

She tossed it to her side of the bed, which was technically the middle, and looked sternly at us once again. "I mean it. It's mine."

It was finally my turn.

"My gift's not as practical as a candle or a pillow," I said. "But it leans into my strengths."

When she opened the box, she looked at me with confusion at first.

It was a little model—a miniature greenhouse I'd built.

"Thank you," she said.

"That's the small one," I explained. "The full-sized version is yours. When you show me where you want it, we'll build it. It can be your studio, a place to paint your rocks, where the light comes in from every angle. I didn't know you when I made it, but I figured maybe you'd want to make teas or something—but now... I think you need an art room."

She threw her arms around me and held me tight.

"I suppose I should probably give you your present now," she said with a mischievous little smile.

"It's not our birthday," I teased.

207

"That's true. But this is a pretty good present. I didn't want to wait until Christmas. Pretty sure I couldn't actually hide it that long."

She reached into her dress pocket and pulled out a long piece of plastic.

It wasn't until she turned it over that I knew what her gift was. It had two blue lines.

"Are you...are you having our young?" Wilder's eyes never left the pregnancy test.

"That's good, right?" she said.

My heart nearly exploded.

"Oh my gods," I whispered. "That...it's everything."

All three of us wrapped our arms around us, tears flowing freely. We were going to be fathers.

Chapter Twenty-Eight

Rumor

"I think you're a mermaid," I whispered, twisting the rock around, making sure I got it right. Right. I slowly rotated it, and, when it was finally facing the correct direction, I realized I was right. This rock was meant to be a mermaid.

I put it down on the table and got my paints to create my palette. My stomach tightened.

I'd been really lucky this entire pregnancy. No morning sickness, no backaches, no swollen feet. But today, my stomach was off. Like someone was squeezing it.

"Maybe you're a mermaid tomorrow," I told the rock, patted it, and walked out of my art studio—the one Vargas had made for me—and waddled back toward the animals to see what Wilder was up to.

And yes, I was at the point of waddling.

I still had two weeks of this pregnancy left, at least if I went to my due date. I didn't know how it was going to go. My mom went early because she had twins, and that was all I had to go by. And it wasn't like I could call her and ask. That part of my life was over and done with.

Most of the time, I didn't care. I was happier here than I'd ever been there. But sometimes, like this— when I needed maternal advice—it hurt.

Wilder was collecting my quail eggs when I got there. He insisted I not do it while I was pregnant. I didn't think there were technically any rules about pregnant women and eggs, but in his mind, if we couldn't be around cat messes, we shouldn't be around chicken messes either. Or quail. Or any other critters. So he took over that task. I stopped arguing after two days. It wasn't a battle I could win, especially not when he had my other mates on his side.

We'd built up a really good customer base of people who wanted the little eggs. I liked them, always had. They were delicious and added something special to a lot of different meals. I just hadn't realized how popular they were.

"Hey, mate. You having a good day?" I leaned against the fence.

"I am, except for Wilder the quail. He's kind of being a pain in the ass."

Wilder liked to escape. And was quite good at it.

"Need my help?"

"No, I'm good. How are you? You look... I don't know, not uncomfortable, but maybe—"

"No, it's uncomfortable. My stomach's not great. I think I might go in and lie down." I could use the nap either which way.

"If you wait a second, I'll walk you in," he offered.

"I'll meet you up there." I had a feeling if I stood still too long, getting going again would be rough.

Halfway to the house, I ran into Penn, holding six jars of honey.

"Give me some of those." I took three from him. "You don't want to drop them."

"Did I drop them?" he asked.

"Not yet." I stuck my tongue out at him. "Is this all for us?"

211

"It is. I have some plans. Some baking plans."
Unless those plans included baklava for the entire
village, he still had overstocked for us.

"That's an awful lot of honey for baking plans."

"Did I mention there were a lot?"

My stomach was now really hurting. "I'm going
up to bed. I want to lie down."

"Did you want company?"

"Maybe. Maybe I need a wolf."

"I got you."

I continued my waddle all the way to my room and
climbed into my nest, hugging my down pillow to my
chest and closing my eyes. I didn't fall asleep until
Penn joined me in his wolf form, his back pressed to
mine, giving me a little bit of support and a whole lot
of love.

When I woke up, it was because the pain had
gotten worse, and I gave a little yelp.

"Are you okay?" Wilder was in the doorway.

"Yeah. I just...yeah."

There was a lick on the back of my neck.

"Penn. I know you're there."

"Honey, need more company?" Wilder asked.

"I'd love some."

He stripped his clothes and took his wolf and joined us on the bed.

The next time I woke up, Vargas was there, too, his wolf at the end of the bed, guarding the door, the position he tended to take when in this form.

I pushed to get up—and the bed was wet. Gross.

I climbed out to see what was happening, and the wolves all stood at attention, giving low growls, their eyes trained on the door.

"Cut it out, you guys. I just—I think I peed the bed." There'd been a time I'd have been embarrassed to have said that, but now, out it came, no blushing or anything. "No one is coming to bother me."

One by one, they shifted back.

"Let me hold your hand when I tell you this, Rumor," Penn said, "but I don't think that's pee. I think it's baby time. That's your water breaking."

"Do you need a midwife?" Vargas was already fishing through his clothes for his phone.

I shook my head. I didn't want any strangers here. I only wanted family.

"No. I need Lily." She'd been there for other omegas' births. She could be there for mine.

Vargas ran out of the room, not even getting dressed. Poor Lily—things she was gonna have to deal with today.

She came up right away and took me to shower while the guys fixed up the bed.

We had a tentative plan for this birth—not that babies cared what our plans were, but when I came back, they had everything set up the way I'd asked.

The tightening in my stomach was now extremely painful. And very frequent.

I'd been having contractions all day without realizing it. I'd brushed them off, thinking they were a stomachache or a pulled muscle.

There was no denying it now. This baby was coming. And soon.

They helped me onto the bed. I wanted to have my wolves with me when I gave birth. For some reason, it felt important that they were front and center and, when I said as much, all three shifted back, without hesitation.

I had the best mates.

Vargas lay above my head, Wilder and Penn on either side of me, as Lily coached me through my labor the way the midwife and experience had taught her.

It was hard. Scary. Overwhelming. But with her guiding my breath and the warmth of my mates' wolves surrounding me, I knew I could do it.

"It's time to push," Lily said, after I screamed about it burning.

I didn't know what I'd thought delivering a baby would be like, but it wasn't this. More than once, I feared I wasn't going to be able to do it. But I had to, there was no other way. It wasn't like I could asked the baby nicely to come out a secret passageway.

This burning, this pulling, this aching—it was too much.

I wasn't sure I could do it. What if my fears were warranted?

"You've got this, Mama. You're so strong. You are the strongest person I know. One push for me." Lily's calm voice gave me the strength I needed.

I sucked in a full breath and pushed with all my might.

When I heard the scream of our little girl for the first time, tears of joy fell down my face—all the pain all but forgotten, my heart filled with so much love.

Lily cleaned her up and put her on my chest, latching on for her first meal like a pro.

My wolves all looked at her, eyes wide.

"You can come back now, guys."

They took their skins and took turns, each of them telling me how beautiful she was. How much they loved me.

"What's her name?" Lily asked.

"Her name is Bernadette. It means strong and brave as a bear." Alpha, omega, or beta, I didn't care. She was going to be the woman the Goddess designed her to be, and I would spend every day showing her how brave, strong, and wonderful she was. She wasn't going to get a childhood like mine.

"Just like our mate." Penn kissed my cheek.

"Just like our mate," the other two mirrored back.

I was only brave and strong because they showed me I could be.

"I love you, mates of mine. Thank you for buying me that day. No backsies."

"No backsies!"

Want to keep up with the omegas and their alpha packs? One-click *Knot My Omega* today!

An Excerpt from *Knot My Omega*

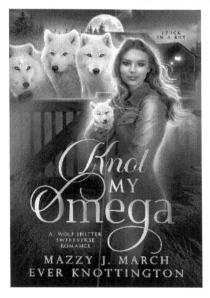

I used to think I'd never find a place where I belonged, and now that I have, they want to take me away.

Life was so much easier when I knew my place, when I understood that I would never be more than a servant, a lowly omega. That was before I was rescued from my pack. Now I'm living a life of freedom, respect, and friendship. Everything I could ever dream of, right? Some days I wonder.

At least I have the farmer's market. Every week, I help sell our pack's goods, eat delicious food, and chat with customers. It's the highlight of my week. That is until three alphas show up and proclaim that I am theirs.

I turn them down. I can't risk it. I know how omegas are treated, and I'd rather have a life of loneliness than one where I'm second class. They accept my rejection sort of.

Every week one of them shows up with a gift, a kind gesture, a smile. They call it wooing, I call it a pain in the ass. Only, truth be told, I kind of like it.

Knot My Omega is the second in the Stuck in a Rut shifter why choose sweetverse romances. Each stand-alone novel features an omega female and her brutish, brooding wolf shifter alphas. Knot My Omega features an omega strong enough to tame the wildest beast, the chance encounter that flips her world upside down, a misunderstood pack, omegaverse goodies including heat, rutting, marking, perfuming, slick, and all the knotty goodness you love. And, of course, a happy ever after that includes an adorable baby or two.,

Made in the USA
Columbia, SC
07 June 2025

59068676R00138